Best Vacation that Never Was

Lynn Lorenz

Best Vacation that Never Was

Originally published in 2009 by LooseId

Available in PDF, EPUB, and Mobi
Editor: Georgia A. Woods
Cover Artist: Lex Valentine/Winterheart Design
Printed in the United States of America

establishments, events, or locales is entirely coincidental.

Warning

This e-book contains sexually explicit scenes and adult language and may be considered offensive to some readers. It is intended for sale to adults ONLY, as defined by the laws of the country in which you made your purchase. Please store your files wisely, where they cannot be accessed by under-aged readers.

* * * * *

DISCLAIMER: Please do not try any new sexual practice, especially those that might be found in BDSM/fetish titles without the guidance of an experienced practitioner. The author will not be responsible for any loss, harm, injury or death resulting from use of the information contained in any of its titles.

About this Title

Genre: LGBT Erotic Contemporary

When Troy Hastings' plans for the vacation of his dreams literally goes up in smoke, he's left homeless, alone, and wearing only a hospital gown. Jason Cooper, the firefighter who rescues him, can only think of what he'd like to do to Troy. Troy's lost everything and Jason wants to help him get his life back. With each passing day, Jason wants that life to include him. But he only has seven days until Troy's friends return from the trip to make Troy see that Jason is the man he's been looking for all along.

Jason spends that time giving Troy the best vacation he's ever had, and in the process, wooing the man who has nothing to lose and everything to gain. Troy's having the time of his life, enjoying stepping out of his comfort zone, trying new things: like a little bondage, the hottest sex he's ever had, and parasailing, and he's game for more.

When the week is up, Troy will find himself a new apartment...unless Jason can convince him to stay.

Publisher's Note: This book contains explicit sexual content, graphic language, and situations that some readers may find objectionable: Anal play/intercourse, male/male sexual practices.

Contents

Chapter One

"**I** don't care what you say; this trip is going to be just what my relationship with Douglas needs to push it to the next level." Troy held the cell phone to his ear with his shoulder as he crammed the last of his toiletries into his shaving kit.

"That's just it, Troy. You don't *have* a relationship with Douglas. All you have are a couple of fucks." Troy could always depend on his best friend Carlton to speak frankly, but frankly, this was *not* what he wanted to hear.

"*Great* fucks." Troy's body tingled just thinking about the three times he and Douglas had done the dirty deed.

"But only fucks. The best you can say is that you're friends with benefits."

"But that's going to change. This cruise is perfect. The romantic nights, the ocean, the exotic ports of call."

"*If* you can keep that alley cat Douglas in your room. Good luck with that." Carlton snorted. "You'll have to tie him to the bed."

"That sounds like fun. Maybe he could tie me up. I should pack a few ties." Troy dashed to the closet, pulled two silk neckties out, folded them, and put them into one of his bags and zipped it up.

Carlton sighed. "Look. I just don't want you hurt, you know. You've been in lust with Douglas since you met him a year ago, and nothing's come of it."

"Of course something's come of it. There's something *special* between us, Carl. I can feel it." Troy lugged the suitcase to the living room and placed it next to the other one and headed back to the bedroom.

"If there was, don't you think Douglas would do something about it? I'm going to tell you this because you're my best friend and I love you." Carlton paused, and Troy braced for the blow he knew was coming. "He's just not that into you."

Troy sank onto the bed and took a deep breath. "That's why this trip is so important. It's my chance to have him all to myself. To make him fall in love with me."

There was silence, then a chuckle. "Well, if anyone could make a man fall for him, it's you, Troy. You're incredible. Smart. Witty. A gorgeous guy with a heart of gold. Shit, Douglas isn't good enough for you, in my opinion."

Rolling his eyes, Troy said, "Yes, Dad. No one's good enough for your little boy."

Carlton laughed. "Damn straight."

"Well, here's a news flash. Your little boy wants Douglas, and he's going to get him. This week. Trust me; Douglas isn't going to know what hit him. When I get off that boat in seven days, it's going to be on Douglas's arm, and he's going to be so in love with me he'll be making reservations for a honeymoon suite in New Hampshire."

"For your sake, I hope so." Carlton sighed.

"Wish you were coming with us. It won't be the same without you." That was the one thing that sucked about the cruise; all his friends, except Carlton, were going.

"No can do. My flight leaves in"—a pause, then the swearing started—"forty-five minutes! Shit, the fucking cab is stuck in fucking traffic, and I can see the sign for the fucking airport just ahead."

"Hey, do you kiss your mother with that mouth?" Troy laughed. "Say hello to your mom for me." If Troy hadn't booked the cruise, he'd also be on the plane to Seattle to hang out with Carlton's family for the holidays, but the chance for a once-in-a-lifetime dream vacation with Douglas was too much to resist.

"She's going to miss you, but she'll understand. Driver! Can't we get out of this mess?" Carlton shouted into the phone.

Troy winced, then laughed. "Don't worry, you'll make it."

"Mom'll kill me if I miss the flight. She's sending a car to pick me up. Look, I'm going to get off the phone so I can yell at the traffic, the driver, and anyone else foolish enough to get in my way. It won't be pretty."

"Okay. See you in seven days."

"Have fun, Troy. And for what it's worth, I hope you get the man you deserve." Carlton hung up.

Troy stared at the phone. What had Carlton meant by that? He shrugged, flipped his cell shut, and tossed it on the bed.

He glanced at the clock. Nearly nine p.m. and there was still so much to do before he left. He stood and looked over his checklist. He'd called for the cab to pick him up at five in the morning, an ungodly hour, but he needed to be at the dock in

Galveston by eight to load his luggage and go through security.

He'd given his neighbor Mrs. Samms the spare key to his apartment so she could water his plants and collect his mail. His cruise tickets, passport, and itinerary were in his carry-on bag sitting on top of his two matching pieces of luggage.

He opened the door to his closet and pulled out the clothes he'd wear tomorrow. Light oatmeal-colored linen trousers, a loose cotton shirt, and a hemp belt, with a matching linen jacket. He'd gone with the lighter colors to set off his new tan.

He stared at himself in the full-length mirror on the back of the closet door, then shrugged off his white terry cloth robe. It pooled like a cloud around his feet on the floor. He'd paid good money over the last four months to build up that sun-kissed glow in a tanning salon, and now it was going to pay off.

He'd gone for an all-over tan. Not a single line marred his body. He turned and checked out his ass in the mirror. Perfect. Plump. Tanned.

If that didn't drive Douglas wild, he didn't know what would. He'd seen the way Douglas had looked at other men, especially men with darker skin. So in

Troy's plan to get his man, getting a tan had been one of the first things he'd done.

He ran his hand over his abs and flat belly and turned to the side, stretching his back leg out like he'd seen so many cover models do.

"Fine as frog's hair," he whispered. His eyes dropped to his cock. "And hung like a horse." He flicked his dick with his finger, and the brief sting shot up its length and into his balls.

He chuckled and, naked, entered the bathroom to start his bath. Just an hour or so soaking in a hot tub of scented water would do him a world of good and take some of the tension out of his shoulders.

Really, there was no reason to be so tense. He had it all under control.

His dream vacation was just ten hours away.

* * * * *

The cigarette dangled from the old man's lips. The television blared. The bottle of whiskey he'd emptied lay on the floor next to his recliner.

He snorted in his sleep.

The cigarette fell, rolled down his belly, and came to rest on his thigh. The embers flared, burned a hole in his flannel pajama bottoms, and seared his skin.

"Fuck."

Half-awake, still drunk, he swatted at the pain, knocking the still-burning cigarette to the floor. It rolled across the bare linoleum and landed next to the rug under the couch.

The cheap cotton rug smoked, smoldered, then ignited.

* * * * *

"I'm not getting out of this tub until the hot water is gone and I look like a prune."

Troy closed his eyes, inhaled, and then exhaled, taking in the calming scents of the too-generous dose of aromatherapy salts he'd dumped into the bath. The water in the tub was the perfect temperature, the candles he'd lit gave off a soft glow, and he sank deeper in the water, letting go of the tightness in his body.

He could just imagine the look of lust on his face when Douglas first saw him, how he'd wonder if Troy's tan was all over. He couldn't wait until Douglas explored every inch of his body to discover if it was.

Carlton was all wrong. Troy wasn't fooling himself; he knew exactly the kind of man Douglas was. The kind who fucked around, but during this vacation, that was going to change.

No more alley cat.

Douglas would be eating out of Troy's hand and purring like a kitten.

* * * * *

The edge of the worn, floral-patterned couch caught fire; hungry red tongues of flame ate their way up the front, devouring the cushions, and then unsatisfied, leaped to the drapes behind them. As they ignited, black smoke in unrelenting hot billows rolled upward to meet the ceiling and then spread across it.

The temperature in the room skyrocketed as the fire attacked the far wall.

The old man's lungs filled with black smoke. He coughed and fell forward out of the chair, landing on the warmer-than-usual floor.

"Shit!" Coughing, gasping, near-blind, and desperate for air, he crawled on trembling hands and knees toward the door. Greedy, unmerciful, the fire took possession of the room, filling it with thick black smoke and lung-scorching heat.

The old man collapsed two feet from the door.

The entire room seemed to groan, held its breath, and then surrendered to the red and black hell of a flashover.

Slender orange fingers, searching for more oxygen to feed on, wound their way through the thin walls between apartments and found fresh fuel next door.

* * * * *

All the tension left Troy's body as he soaked.

He sighed.

This, and Douglas, was all he needed. Okay, not really *all*, but having Douglas would be a great start.

He'd fallen for the man the first time they'd met. Douglas had been a friend of a friend in Troy's little group of friends, five gay men in their thirties who enjoyed spending time together, eating, clubbing, and dissecting their love lives. They'd called themselves the Breakfast Club because they'd met one morning at a diner after a hard night of clubbing. Troy and Carlton, two queen-size sheets to the wind, had staggered into the diner, spotted Tom, Mark, and Mel sitting in a large booth looking equally wasted, and laughing, they'd joined them. The rest, as they say, is history.

It had been the five of them for three years. Then last year Mel had introduced Douglas to the group, and that was all she wrote for Troy.

Douglas had movie-star good looks and knew it. And he was a man-whore of the first caliber. And Troy should know one when he saw one, because he'd been a slut too.

But when Troy met Douglas, he'd given up his man-chasing ways. And gladly. Troy had found his man. Unfortunately, Douglas hadn't gotten the memo. He remained an alley cat, footloose, free of all entanglements, making the rounds to eat off the proverbial laps of different lovers.

After six months, Troy had finally maneuvered Douglas into showing up at his apartment, alone. It didn't take much more than Troy's opening a bottle of wine, pouring two glasses, and handing one to Douglas. Douglas took a sip as Troy leaned forward, trailed his finger down Douglas's ripped chest, and over one hard nipple.

"Let's fuck," Troy whispered.

Chapter Two

Unsatisfied, the fire ate the wall between the apartments and continued on. One arm of it attacked the ceiling, as the other one extended across the antique wool ten-by-twelve Turkish rug, gobbling up every strand of hand-knotted, hand-dyed yarn.

The designer leather love seat and the secondhand teak coffee table, including a collector's autographed edition of turn-of-the-century photographs of naked men, were devoured like appetizers at a cheap happy hour. The fire moved on and rapidly consumed the luggage that, like two soldiers, blocked the way to the bedroom and small bath.

Black superheated smoke flowed along the twelve-foot ceiling and banked. The thermal layer moved lower, filled the space, and touched the small round plastic device on the wall near the kitchen.

* * * * *

Troy opened his eyes to a loud, insistent, and very unfamiliar blaring. He sat up in the tub, sloshing water over the sides, and looked around.

Was that the smoke detector?

"Couldn't be." He hadn't left anything on in the apartment. Nothing cooking. No candles lit except in here. He looked at them, then decided they weren't the problem.

He sniffed the air like a dog.

"Shit! That's smoke!" He surged out of the tub and grabbed a towel. Dripping water across the tile floor, he rushed to the door.

Gray smoke, thin and hesitant, as if it had a secret, seeped under the bathroom door.

Troy grabbed the doorknob. "Fuck!"

Pain shot through him like he'd touched a hot pan's unprotected handle on the stove. He shook his hand, gave it a quick look, then went to the sink and turned on the taps. Holding his hand under the water, he grimaced as the pain subsided.

Smoke wound around his knees like a cat, and he coughed. The room had become a sauna, hot, moist heat baking him. He'd never liked saunas.

Somehow, unbelievably, his apartment was on fire.

Adrenaline exploded through his body like an orgasm.

Fight or flight?

No choice. He needed to get the hell out of there. Panic built like a coiled spring as Troy scanned the small bath. The window over the tub was his only exit.

Blinking back tears, he scooped up the towel he'd let drop to the floor and plunged it into the bathtub of water, then pulled it out. Slinging the sopping terry cloth around his waist, Troy's hands shook as he jerked another towel off the bar next to the sink and doused it in the tub.

Coughing, he wiped his face, then flung the soaking towel over his head. After climbing up on the tub, he balanced on the edge as he flipped open the locks and pushed the window up.

Wisps of gray escaped before he could get the window open wide enough to crawl out. His eyes watered, nose ran, and sweat dripped. He wiped his face again. The towel wasn't as wet as it had been just a moment ago.

The sauna had disappeared. He was trapped in a fucking oven.

And he was going to die. Burn to death.

Heart slamming in his chest, he and the smoke vied for the small space of the open window. He got his legs through and sat on the ledge. Twisting his body, he maneuvered his shoulders and head out, and at last he gulped down clean air.

He looked down. Eyes watering so badly he could barely see, he coughed and his body trembled. He didn't need to see to know he was three floors up.

Every muscle, every nerve, every fiber in his body, and every neuron fired in his mind, screaming at him to jump. To leap. To fly. To just get the fuck away from being burned alive.

Troy sat on the windowsill, refusing to obey.

Even as one part of his mind tried to kill him, another part kept him alive.

Behind him, a burst of heat seared the bare skin on his back. Too terrified to look, knowing the bathroom would soon be in flames, he shifted farther out onto the ledge.

Sirens in the distance.

Nearly blind, choking, he wept. He would be rescued. He just had to hold on.

Troy cleared away the mixture of sweat and tears dripping down his face with the now-dry towel and looked down. A small ledge ran along the bottom of the window, nothing more than a row of bricks standing out from the facade. Nothing more than a toehold.

He took a deep breath, twisted, and holding on to the sill, faced the building and stared through the window. Hell burned on the other side of his bathroom door, outlining the flimsy barrier in bright red.

He had to move. Now.

Fingers clinging onto what little purchase he could find, barefoot, he flattened his body against the bricks and stepped onto the thin ledge as if it were a tightrope and he were a fucking Wallenda.

* * * * *

Every time Jason rode the engine to a call, it was a wild rush. This was something he never wanted to get used to. Maybe when he was old and gray. Hell, maybe never. He'd done a lot of crazy shit in his life, but this? It didn't get any better.

He glanced from the backseat of the cabin of the pride of Engine Company Twenty-Five to his boss, Lieutenant Alan Morris, riding shotgun. Eyes closed and head nodding as he slept, the man looked like he could be on a Sunday drive with the family, instead of in a forty-foot-long ladder truck on his way to a two-alarm fire.

"*Yeeehaaww*!" Jason whooped, just to get the old man going.

"Shit, Cooper. I was taking a nap." Morris groaned and tipped his helmet over his face.

"Coming up now!" The driver's voice crackled over their headsets. "Get ready to rock and roll!" In the background, Jason heard the driver notifying command of their arrival and switching to the tactical channel for communications.

Jason snapped his chin strap to the helmet and grinned at the man sitting behind Morris, a new recruit named Tom. The twenty-one-year-old had that gleam in his eyes, as if he'd just been told he was going to be let loose in a candy store with a shopping cart, and it was all fucking free.

He reached out and slapped the guy's arm. "Take the controls this time." Morris opened his eyes and gave Jason a nod. Jason returned a wink.

"No shit? I get to launch the ladder?"

"If we need it, sure. No better experience than in the field." Jason knew you could practice this at the training facility until you had it down pat, but nothing beat having to perform in an actual fire.

The sirens of the other units, police, fire, with a couple of ambulances thrown in, filled the night air and made the only music he danced to. His heart beat faster as the adrenaline in his system ratcheted up a notch. Man, there was nothing better to climb the ladder with than colored lights strobing off the glass of the surrounding buildings. Hell, it was his personal dance club.

And he was here for the party.

The truck slowed, then came to a stop near the first available hydrant, the doors opened. Jason swung out of the cabin with Tom right behind him, and they ran to the back of the truck. After pulling out the hose, they slung it around the hydrant and motioned for the truck to continue up to its position near the building, deploying the rest of the hose. He and Tom worked like a two-man precision drill team to break the cap and attach to hose to the hydrant. That done, they trotted up to the back of their parked truck. They might not use the water, but they had to be connected just in case.

At the rear of the ladder truck, Tom joined him at the controls.

"What do we have?" he asked.

Jason surveyed the building. "Holy mother of God." He gave a low, soft whistle.

Flames erupted from windows along the entire third floor, and the fourth floor, the building's top floor, had at least two units burning. It wouldn't be long before that entire floor was engulfed too.

"They're going to have to roll to a four alarm." That would bring in the neighboring fire districts.

Police held back the crowd as members of the other fire units' search teams entered the burning building. Cops and firemen evacuated the adjoining buildings, emptying men, women, and children onto the streets. The cops moved them to a safe location down the block but kept them herded together for a head count.

To the untrained eye, it might have looked like chaos, but to Jason, it was a well-choreographed ballet. Half a dozen vehicles disgorged massive long hoses from their back ends like giant insects giving birth, as his counterparts raced to nearby hydrants, broke the caps, hooked up the hoses, and opened the valves. As a rolling wave of water filled each hose, they came to life, powerful snakes being charmed by men and women trained to handle them.

Tom pointed. "Up there. Shit. Is that a man?"

Jason's gaze followed Tom's arm. He squinted through the haze of smoke and embers.

"Fuck."

Halfway between two windows spewing flames, a man clung like a fly to the side of the building.

"What the hell is he holding on to?" Tom shouted.

"I don't know, but we're going for him." Jason slapped Tom's helmet and jerked his thumb up. Like a precision drill team, Tom and he went into action, lowering the four hydraulic stabilizers in place to keep the rig from tipping over. Once that was done, he watched as Tom rotated the ladder into position.

Jason counted the seconds as the ladder unfolded, one section sliding out at a time. And taking way too long. He stared up at the man, assessing him.

Strong back muscles corded with effort, the skin covering them slick with sweat and black from smoke or maybe burns. *Fuck.* Head to the side, long arms outstretched, and fingers gripped brick to hold him in place.

He wore nothing but a towel wrapped around his narrow waist, covering an ass

that Jason wanted to see naked. *Oh shit.*
Some of the guys laughed about getting
hard just being in the midst of the action at
a fire; hell, he'd experienced it himself. But
damn, he wasn't supposed to get hard
looking at someone he was about to rescue.

Once the ladder extended far enough
to reach their target, Jason began his
climb. Halfway up, he called out to the
man, "Fire department. I'm coming to get
you. Hold on."

"What the fuck do you think I'm
doing?" the guy yelled back, then coughed.

With an attitude like that, Jason knew
the guy would be all right.

"Almost to you."

"Hurry. Please."

This time Jason heard the fear in the
guy's voice. "I'm going to help you onto the
ladder; then you're going to have to climb
down. Do you think you can do that?" At
the top of the ladder now, Jason reached up
and touched the man's calf.

"Yes. I can do that." He nodded.

"I'm going to climb up over you, then
back you down onto the ladder."

The man coughed and nodded again.
Jason climbed higher on the ladder and put
his gloved hands on the man's waist, but
they slid off sweat-slicked skin.

"Shit." He wiped his gloves off on the towel, brushing the backs of the guy's thighs.

"Hey. Don't get fresh. We haven't been introduced." The man choked. He leaned his head against the heated bricks. "Just get me down." He shuddered.

"It's going to be okay, man. I got you." Jason took him by the waist and eased him back. "Step back. Put your foot on the rung of the ladder."

"Okay." He took his foot off the ledge, and his hands slid down the bricks. "Don't let me fall." His foot, still on the ledge, trembled, and Jason felt it through the man's straining body.

Jason pressed into his back to let him know he was right there. "I've got you. Feel me? I'm not going to let you fall."

Coughing, the man lowered himself, sliding down the front of Jason's jacket, his ass pressing against Jason's groin. Jesus he shouldn't be turned on, but he was. How twisted was that?

Jason wrapped one arm around the man's body and held him as he got both feet onto the ladder.

"Now, we go down."

"Okay."

Jason moved his hand over the man's sweat-drenched chest. He couldn't resist pressing against his well-defined pec and wishing he could feel that hard nipple with the bare palm of his hand.

The man reached up and covered Jason's larger, gloved hand with his. And pressed it into his body, keeping Jason right where he was.

Oh shit. He pulled his hand away to grab the handrails of the ladder.

Jason began his descent, one rung at a time, the guy following, his towel-covered bottom just above Jason's head. If Jason reached up, he could jerk the towel off and get a good look at that tight ass. The view of muscular thighs was killing him, keeping him hard.

"Cooper, what's going on up there?" Tom's voice interrupted Jason's randy thoughts, thank God.

"Taking it slow. He's pretty shaky. Want to make sure he gets down."

"Good man."

Jason groaned. He wasn't a good man; he was a horny man.

And he wanted the guy in the towel.

Troy counted every step down. His body shook, either with the strain of hanging on to the building or with relief. He didn't know which one, because right now, his brain wasn't working. He could barely breathe, and if he coughed, he really didn't want to see what he hocked up.

He didn't think he'd be able to make it. His control slipped, his body shook, and he fell forward, clutching the ladder to him. The air around him was so heated, each breath felt as if he were inhaling straight out of a blow-dryer, and he had the mother of all sore throats.

"Are you okay?"

"No. I can't breathe." He gasped. Strong hands, the gloves' thick fabric rough against his skin, slid over his back, dragging along his skin. Even in his state, he understood the touch meant to comfort. He'd be all right. The fireman wouldn't leave him.

"Tom, make sure there's an EMT standing by when we get down. He'll need oxygen. He's sucked in a hell of a lot of smoke," his rescuer ordered.

Troy's trembling subsided as he pulled himself together. "Let's go."

He stepped down, and the firefighter moved with him, matching his steps, never getting too far ahead of him. Troy knew he was safe. He trusted the man helping him not to let him fall.

Troy came off the last rung and stood on solid ground, or at least on the platform of the fire engine. The firefighter guided him over to the steps. Another short climb and he'd be down, off the truck and on the street.

After he stepped off the last stair, he turned to the firefighter, wanting to say something. Their gazes met for the first time, and whatever moisture was left in Troy's mouth evaporated.

The firefighter pushed his helmet back. Blue eyes and a crooked but sexy-as-hell smile greeted him.

Christ, how much smoke did he suck down?

"Come on." Strong arms, those same ones that had stroked him and reassured him that he'd be safe, wrapped around his shoulders and guided him over to the ambulance as the EMT tech walked beside him.

"Take care of him." The firefighter gave him a last lingering touch, his hand running over Troy's bare, sooty shoulder, then left.

The med tech quickly went over Troy's body, checking for any injuries.

"Damn, you're lucky."

Troy gave him a weak smile, motioned to his throat, and tipped his hand near his mouth to indicate he needed a drink.

"I'm sorry. No water until we've checked out any damage in your throat.

But you can use it to cool off." The EMT gave him a bottle of water, and Troy upturned the bottle over his head. "We'll give you intravenous fluids for now."

Damn, that felt so good. He shivered as the water evaporated off his overheated skin.

"Just some scratches and some abrasions." The tech pointed to the stretcher. "Get on."

Troy sat down, his filthy body leaving smears of black soot on the white sheets as he lay back against the raised bed. The EMT placed a mask over his face, and he sucked in oxygen. And immediately choked.

He pushed the mask away as hard coughs racked his body. The tech handed him a towel, and he spit into it. A quick glance at what he'd deposited was all he needed. He groaned, folded the towel, and handed it back. Christ, his head hurt.

Then the mask was shoved back on, the tech encouraging him to breathe as deep as possible. As his breathing eased, he became aware of others around him receiving medical assistance, the emergency vehicles surrounding them, and last, the crowds of bystanders.

Like some kind of weird three-ring circus, lights flickered, bathing everything and everyone in a surreal red and blue. The responding personnel were the performers, and the onlookers the audience. Instead of laughter and cheers, a hushed, almost reverential silence echoed in the street. The smell of smoke, fire, and what had burned singed his nostrils, a bizarre stand-in for the comforting aroma of popcorn and hot dogs.

Mesmerized, he watched black smoke rise above the building like a mini-mushroom cloud from his very own personal Yucca Flats.

Troy's building burned, taking his dream vacation and his entire life with it.

Chapter Three

With the rescue complete, Jason turned to fighting the fire. As he shrugged on his oxygen tanks, put his mask on, and tested his air supply, he couldn't stop thinking about the man from the ledge and the intense reaction he'd had just looking at the guy, much less when he'd touched him.

Forcing those thoughts from his mind, he focused on the task ahead. Not focusing could cost him his life or, worse, the lives of the men and women working with him. They relied on him, just as he relied on them, for survival.

Jason picked up his ax and joined the others entering the still-burning building.

* * * * *

The EMT began to toss the straps over Troy.

Troy moved the air mask. "Hey, what's going on?" he rasped out.

"We're going to transport you to the hospital now."

"Hospital?" Still dazed, Troy didn't want to go to the hospital. He wanted to go home. But home was gone. Shit, his head still hurt. So did his throat. Everything hurt.

"You need to get checked out. You're pretty beat up, and they'll want to give you some lung treatments for the smoke inhalation."

Troy nodded, too weak and too hoarse to fight about it.

The tech tightened the straps, and he and another tech lifted the stretcher into the back of the ambulance and locked it in place. Then one of them climbed up with Troy and settled into a seat as the other guy slammed the back door shut.

With the noise from the outside muffled and the strobe lights of the emergency vehicles dimmed, it was like riding in a peaceful cocoon. Troy listened to his own breathing under the mask, much like being underwater, snorkeling or scuba diving. Eerie but comforting.

And he was too tired to care. He closed his eyes and let exhaustion take him.

* * * * *

Just before dawn, Jason joined his crew back at the ladder truck. All around him the men and women of the different engine companies were putting away their tools, rolling up the hoses, and shutting down operations. A few of the trucks had already left.

The police still monitored the area, and a small crowd, along with several local reporters, hung around. Jason was glad he didn't have to talk to any of them. PR wasn't his thing. He was more of an action kind of guy.

He couldn't forget the guy from the ledge. Damn, it took some real balls to have climbed out of that window and clung to the side of the building. Jason's interest in and respect for the man had catapulted in that single moment.

Knowing the guy had been scared had made it even more incredible. Jason remembered his dad's definition of bravery. *"It's being scared of something, but facing it anyway."*

Jason couldn't doubt the guy's bravery or smarts. He'd obviously had nothing but a towel to wear, and from the looks and feel of it, he'd soaked them in water to stay cool.

He was a man Jason wanted to know more about.

He didn't even wonder if the guy was gay. He'd known it after the first touch and the guy's cocky comment about not being introduced. Not the words of a straight man.

He climbed to the top of the engine and checked out the scene. The ambulance was long gone. Probably took the guy to the hospital. But which one?

Looking back at the charred, still-smoking remains of the building, he knew the man couldn't go home. Maybe he had some friends who'd take him in.

Maybe not.

Really, it wasn't Jason's problem.

So why did he feel responsible for the guy? A complete stranger.

"Let's go, Cooper!" Tom shouted up at him.

"What was the count?" Jason asked as he climbed down and joined the men standing around the rig.

"Three dead," Lieutenant Morris replied. "Early findings say smoke inhalation."

The men nodded. They knew, despite common belief, it was the smoke that killed most people in a fire, not being burned.

The ride back to the station was silent, just brief eye contact and a small nod of the lieutenant's head to tell each of his men that they'd done well. The excitement of the fire eased off. Another job complete; another fire beaten. Tired, but proud of the work he'd done, Jason leaned back against the seat.

There was no need for words.

* * * * *

The lights in the small treatment room Troy lay in had been dimmed. In the hall outside the large glass window, hospital staff bustled back and forth, stretchers carrying new patients rolled past, and concerned family and friends wandered by, looking stunned and lost.

He'd had the oxygen mask replaced by a thin tube up his nose. The automatic blood pressure cuff inflated and deflated with irritating regularity, and his heart monitor softly beeped as the IV continued to drip some clear liquid stuff into his veins to help with dehydration.

His scrapes, scratches, and abrasions had been cleaned and bandaged a couple of hours ago. Like some little kid whose mom had spit-cleaned his face, parts of him were clean, but large parts remained soot covered. He wanted to sit under a shower for a very long time, rinsing away this entire night. A *cold* shower. His skin jumped at the thought of anything hot.

Since he was no longer classified as an emergency, he'd been relegated to an occasional nurse popping in to check his IV and his vitals. After having been given so much attention, a part of him felt neglected.

He should be grateful. He knew it. He was alive and so incredibly fortunate to not have been hurt. Burned. If there hadn't been a ledge and he'd been faced with a choice of jumping from that third-story window or being burned alive, he'd have taken his chances and jumped.

At least it would have been quick.

Troy shuddered.

He'd been given a second chance at life.

Now he just had to figure out what to do with it.

A nurse came in, checked him, and then handed him a clipboard.

"You just need to finish filling out these forms and sign them."

"Okay," he whispered.

"The doctor is releasing you. Good news, right?"

"Good news." He nodded. "What about my throat?"

"It's going to be sore for a while. The doctor wrote you a few prescriptions to help with that, but there's no permanent damage." She handed him a prescription slip. "Once I have those forms, you're free to go."

Troy frowned. "Go where?" He looked down at his hospital gown. "In what?"

"Oh. Isn't there anyone out in the waiting room for you?"

"No." With everything that had happened, Troy hadn't been able to call anyone. "I don't have a phone."

"I'll bring one and plug it in. Then you can call someone to come and get you."

He nodded and went to work on the forms.

Ten minutes later, the nurse returned with a phone and connected it to a wall jack.

"Here you go." She placed the phone on the table next to his bed and took the clipboard from him. "Thanks. I'll bring back your copies soon as I'm done. Then we'll take the IV out."

Troy reached over and picked up the phone.

Before he realized what he'd done, he called Carlton. The phone rang, then went to voice mail. Damn. He'd left for his mother's last night.

What time was it, anyway?

Troy glanced around the room. No clock. He put the phone back down and sat up on the edge of the bed. The room spun a little, but nothing he couldn't handle.

He stood, the floor beneath his feet cool and solid. Grabbing his IV pole with one hand, he clutched his gown shut with the other and then stepped into the hall. At one end were double doors leaving the ward, at the other, a nurses' station.

He walked to the counter. "Excuse me."

A pretty young nurse looked up. "Yes?"

"What time is it?"

She pointed to a large clock on the back of the wall. "Seven thirty."

Even if he could remember his friends' cell phone numbers, it was too late. With no luggage, tickets, passport, or money, all hope of the vacation with Douglas had vanished in a proverbial puff of smoke. But that was the least of his problems.

"Where's the bathroom?"

"Third door on the left." She motioned to it.

He gave her a nod and headed to it. Maybe there was a shower. At least he could get clean. Pushing open the door, he flicked on the light, stepped in, dragging the IV behind him, and closed the door.

No shower. Just a sink and toilet.

He peed, flushed, and then went to the sink. He washed his face, dried it with paper towels, and gave up on his fantasy of a shower. Staring at his face in the mirror, he grimaced as he ran his hand over the stubble on his cheek streaking through the soot, then raked his fingers through his hair in a vain attempt at taming it. He was only making things worse.

In the confines of the small bathroom, the stench from the soot and sweat covering his body filled his nostrils. He choked and then grabbed a length of toilet tissue from the roll and blew his nose until the tissue came away clean. He flushed the used tissue down the toilet.

Troy returned to his room and stared at the bed he'd lain in for most of the night. It was streaked with soot, and he could see a reminder of his body's image on the sheet, as if it were the shroud of Turin.

He sat in the chair next to the bed, pulled the phone into his lap, and stared at it, thinking of whom to call. Carlton's number was the only one he knew by heart. Without his cell phone with his contacts in it, he was screwed.

No home, no phone, no wallet, no money.

No one to turn to.

Oh, he was so screwed.

* * * * *

Jason took down the duty roster and signed out. Another shift done. Another fire fought. They'd been able to save most of the lower floors from burning, but the water damage would be massive. And they'd contained the fire, kept it from spreading to the nearby buildings.

He strolled to his car at the back of the fire station's parking lot and hit the remote. The red Explorer beeped and unlocked. Jason slid in and put his key in the ignition, then just sat there.

Something had been bugging him, and he knew what it was. Well, not what it was, but whom. The guy on the ledge.

His rescue.

Yeah. His. Jason had begun to think about the man in the towel as his.

Where was he now?

He'd been taken to the hospital; Jason knew that. He might not have been badly injured, but he'd have to be checked out.

Jason glanced at the clock on his dash. Seven a.m.

The guy had probably left by now. Discharged. Someone would have come and picked him up. A friend.

A lover.

Jason's stomach clenched at that thought.

Still.

No harm in checking. If he wasn't at the hospital, Jason could stop worrying. He'd be fine. If not? Hell, if he was still there?

Nothing wrong with checking on someone whose life you saved, was there?

Hell no.

Jason turned the key, the car started, and he pulled out of the lot, onto the street and headed to the hospital.

Chapter Four

Jason rushed through the emergency room doors and straight to the counter.

"I'm looking for a guy."

The admitting nurse looked up from the computer screen and nodded. "Name?"

"I don't know his name."

"Okay." The helpful look faded from her face. "Do you have someone special in mind, or are you just looking for any guy?"

"Someone special. He came in last night. From the fire."

"We had several patients from there. Can you be more specific?" Crossing her arms on the counter, she stared up at him, waiting.

Jason grinned. "He was wearing nothing but a towel."

The woman's brows rose. "Seems the towel made a big impression on you."

"You could say that. Look, I'm the firefighter who brought him down, and I just wanted to check on him. See if he's okay." Jason held out his identification card to prove it.

"Sure. How about you go on back, see if you can find him? Wait over there, and I'll buzz you in."

"Great!" Jason bounced on his toes like a teen at his first concert as he waited for the double doors to swing open. They opened outward, and he bolted through them.

Quickly walking down the corridor, Jason looked from side to side, checking out the rooms. Almost to the nurses' station he glanced in the window to a room and halted.

The towel guy sat in a chair, shoulders slumped, staring down at his bare feet.

Jason's heart soared, then broke at the torn look on the guy's face. Sorrow. Regret. Fear. It was the fear that made Jason's stomach knot, made him want to make it better, do whatever it took to put a smile on his face.

He stepped into the doorway. "Hey."

The guy's gaze rose. He focused, blinked, and then his brows furrowed as he took Jason in.

"Hello. Do I know you?" Troy croaked out.

Oh God. Please say I know you.

A smiling god stood in his door. A dark-haired god in dark blue jeans and a baby blue polo shirt that clung to each and every muscle in the man's body. There was something familiar about his blue eyes.

"Not really. I'm the guy," the god said.

Troy swallowed the lump in his throat. The hottest man he'd ever laid eyes on just said hello, and Troy was wearing the ugliest hospital gown on earth. Maybe the universe.

Perfect.

"The guy?" Troy's voice was still hoarse.

"From the fire. The firefighter on the ladder." He bounced the toe of his boot on the floor, looking incredibly adorable and tentative, as he hung half in the room and half out of it.

"That's it!" Troy choked, starting a coughing fit.

"Hey, take it easy." The guy came in the room and poured Troy a cup of water from the pitcher on the table. "Here, take a sip."

Troy took the cup from him, their fingers brushing. The shock wave rolled through his body, and he swallowed hard.

The firefighter's Adam's apple jerked as his eyes widened.

Troy took a sip to hide his reaction, then put it on the table next to the phone.

"Have you been discharged yet?"

"Yeah. All ready to go." Troy sighed.

"Is someone coming for you?" The guy bit his bottom lip.

Troy wanted to bite it for him. Bite it, suck on it, give it a gentle nibble. God, once a slut, always a slut.

"No." Troy shook his head. "I...I don't have my phone. And most of my friends, well, all my friends, are leaving this morning on a cruise."

"A cruise you were supposed to be on?" The man leaned back against the door, looking as if he was going to settle there for a while.

"Yeah. A dream vacation." He frowned. "But all my stuff is gone."

"Shit. I'm sorry about that."

Troy shrugged. "I'm alive."

The other guy's eyes glinted. "Yeah, you are."

Those blue eyes held Troy captive.

Troy cleared his still-sore throat. It hurt to talk so much. "Well, thanks for coming by."

The guy straightened as if to leave. "I don't think we've been introduced. My name is Jason Cooper." He stuck out his hand at Troy.

"Troy Hastings." He slid his hand into Jason's, and they shook. And shook. And shook, as if neither of them would let go.

Jason took a step back, breaking their connection. "Have you got anywhere to go?"

"Not really. Everything I owned, except my car, was in the apartment. I don't even have the keys to my car. Guess they burned up too." He coughed from the exertion of speaking.

Jason bit his lip again. "Look. I know you don't know me, and I know we've just met, but if you want, you could come home with me."

"With you?" Troy gasped. Go home with a god?

"Just until you get on your feet. Get your stuff sorted out, you know." Jason shrugged.

Troy sat back and exhaled. This wasn't for real, was it? Was he in some sort of crazy dream? He didn't know what to do. Didn't know what to do about anything right now.

"I...I...I," he sputtered.

"I'll take that as a yes." Jason came in the room. "Are these your papers?" He tapped the folder on the table.

Troy nodded.

Jason scooped them up, taking control. "Come on. Let's go."

Troy stood and looked down. "No clothes."

"That's okay. Once we get to my place I'll lend you some of mine. I'm guessing we're about the same size." He stepped back to let Troy walk past him out the door.

"Thank you," Troy whispered and followed his rescuer down the hall and out the doors of the emergency room as people stared at him.

Hadn't they ever seen a barefoot man, covered in soot, wearing a hospital gown before?

"My car is parked outside."

They reached the car, a bright red Explorer. Troy barked a silent laugh.

"Yeah, I know. Red. Firefighter. Fire engines are red." Jason shrugged, but it was unapologetic. "It's cliché, but there you have it."

"It suits you."

Troy opened the car door and looked at the spotless gray leather seats. "I'm filthy."

He glanced across at Jason through the open door.

"No problem." Jason disappeared from sight; the rear hatch opened and then slammed shut. Jason reappeared at the driver's door and tossed a blanket across the console. "Here you go."

"Thanks." Troy arranged it over his seat and then climbed in, careful not to get any of the soot on the car.

The seat felt so much better than the hospital chair. His body ached and his lungs hurt when he took deep breaths, but the nurse had told him that would go away in a few days. Troy sank back, closed the door, and put on the seat belt.

Jason started the Explorer, and they pulled out of the parking lot.

For one brief moment, Troy thought maybe he was out of his mind. He'd gotten into a car with a complete stranger, and he had no idea where they were going.

He glanced across at Jason. What would Carlton say about this?

Have you lost your mind? You don't even know him! He could be a serial killer!

But serial killers weren't this nice, were they? Besides, he and Jason weren't complete strangers. They'd met before. Outside his building. Three floors up.

Troy fell asleep rationalizing his answers to Carlton.

*****

Fingers feathered over his cheek. Troy turned into them as a soft moan escaped his lips.

"Hey, man. Wake up. We're home."

Troy inhaled. A warm, musky scent, clean with a touch of citrus, filled his senses. Then the sharp odor of smoke overpowered the other smell, and he opened his eyes.

And focused on light blue eyes, thick dark lashes, full lips, and a chin with a boyish dimple. His hero.

"Jason?" he rasped.

"You remembered my name!" Jason grinned. "We're home. Uh, my place." He stepped back, and Troy looked around.

He sat in the Explorer, the door open. Jason stood next to it waiting for him to get out. Troy slid off the seat and stood clutching his hospital gown closed.

"I got a space right outside the apartment." Jason bounced like an excited puppy.

"That's good, right?" Troy raised his eyebrows.

"Very. Good karma." Jason nodded.

"You believe in karma?" Troy asked as he followed Jason's jean-clad ass to his apartment door.

"Yep." Jason put his key in the lock, and the door swung open. He stepped in, and Troy watched as he punched in some numbers on the alarm pad.

"Me too."

"Cool." Jason nodded.

They stared at each other as the moment dragged on.

"Well, this is my place. It's not much. I'm saving up for a house." Jason waved his hand to indicate the apartment, and Troy nodded.

It wasn't very different from his place. Or how his place had been.

Warm brown leather furniture and bookcases. Lots and lots of bookcases. Filled with books, trinkets, and photos. At the other end was a galley kitchen. Everything was neatly put away, not even a glass left out. A small raised café table with two stools sat in front of double French doors that led to a small patio.

"It's nice." Troy smiled.

Jason smiled back. Bit his lip.

Troy's heart stuttered at the tentative, uncertain gesture.

"I really need a bath," he rasped.

"Sure, man. Of course." Jason rushed to a door and flung it open. "This is my bedroom. The bath's through there."

Troy slipped past him, positive he might not be able to control himself if they touched again. And if he flung himself on Jason, smelling so bad, Troy wouldn't blame the guy for pushing him away. Right now, he couldn't take a rejection, not on top of what he'd been through last night. But Christ, it would feel so good to be held, if only for a little while.

"Thanks." He opened the door.

"Use whatever you need. I have extra razors in the cabinet."

Troy ducked in.

"And there's a toothbrush in there too."

Troy popped his head back out. "Okay."

"And I'll get you something to wear while you're bathing."

"Thanks." Troy grinned and shut the door before Jason could say another word.

"Shit." Jason smacked himself upside his head. "Stupid. Stupid. Stupid." He'd sounded like an idiot the way he blathered when he was nervous. And he was usually nervous around attractive guys. All his macho self-confidence, all his bravura, faded into a fumbling mess as he reverted to the shy sixteen-year-old he'd been just thirteen years ago.

The shower turned on.

Jason turned to his dresser and pulled open the bottom drawer. Jerking out a pair of navy sweats and a T-shirt, he tossed them on his bed for Troy. Then he pulled open the top drawer and stared down at his underwear.

He couldn't give him a pair of underwear he'd worn. And he didn't have a fresh pack. And he didn't know if Troy wore briefs or boxers. Cotton or silk.

He pushed the drawer shut.

Troy would have to go commando until they could go shopping for clothes.

Leaving the bedroom, Jason went to the kitchen, pulled out a pad of paper and a pen, and sat at the table to make a list of the things Troy would need to replace.

Driver's license. Credit cards. Money. Clothes.

And entire apartment.

Jason frowned as he looked around his own place.

Pictures of his family and friends peppered the bookcases. He might be able to replace some of them; his parents were still alive. But what about Troy? Could he replace treasured photos, memories of his life and childhood?

Jason's gaze came to rest on the baseball he'd hit a home run with to win the big game his senior year of high school.

He could never replace the dried rose his first gay date had given him on New Year's Eve the year he turned twenty.

Or his little sister's first clay piece, an ashtray? She'd given it to him for his sixteenth birthday, right in front of his parents, giving away the hidden truth that he'd been smoking.

Everything like that in Troy's life had been destroyed.

And why should that matter to Jason? And what the hell was he doing bringing a man home? For all Jason knew, Troy could be a serial killer.

Chapter Five

Troy stood under the cool shower, rinsing as much of the soot off as possible before taking the bar of Zest to his battered body. He lathered it in his hands and, taking a deep breath, smoothed it over his skin.

It stung, but he kept on scrubbing, working the soap to a lather in his hands, then attacking a part of his body. Arms. Legs. Chest. Everywhere the bandages didn't cover. Even his groin wept liquid soot. Black water swirled down the drain just like the scene in *Psycho*, his own form of bloodletting.

At last the water ran clear.

He opened his mouth and stood under the showerhead, swallowing water until his parched throat had been soothed and his burning thirst had been slaked. The water bubbled up in his throat and ran down his chin.

After turning the water off, he stood there, dripping dry. The thought of a rough towel against his skin scared him more than using the soap. He stepped out onto a plush mat next to the tub and took down a towel.

They were soft, thank God. He buried his face in it and inhaled. Smelled good too. He rubbed it over his head, drying his hair, then his shoulders, and slowly, carefully, patted the rest of his body dry.

At the sink, he stared into the mirror. Much better. Emerging from beneath a black beast stood a man. Scruffy but clean.

Now where was that razor and toothbrush?

After shaving and brushing his teeth, Troy sagged against the sink. Exhaustion threatened to steal the bones from his legs, but he stiffened them. He peeked out of the bathroom and saw the clothes Jason had left for him on the bed. The door to the bedroom had been shut. Moving slower than a sloth, Troy went to the bed and sat on the edge to pull on the sweatpants and T-shirt.

After dressing, he just sat. Standing seemed impossible, but he took a deep breath and pushed to his feet.

They fit, but the shirt was a little big. Jason and he were about the same height, but Jason had more muscle mass, especially in his arms and legs. Probably from hoisting all the firefighting equipment.

Troy left the bedroom and found him sitting at the small dining table.

"Hi."

Jason looked up and smiled. "Hi. Feel better?"

"Yeah. Thanks." Troy didn't know what to say. He certainly couldn't ask all the questions he had or tell all his worries about what he'd do about the fire. Or talk about the disappointment of not going on the cruise and missing the opportunity to be with Douglas.

No, that would take too much energy, and right now he didn't have enough, not even to keep standing there. He slumped onto the couch.

"Are you hungry? Can I fix you some breakfast?" Jason stood and headed to the kitchen.

"No. Please. I really just want to sleep. I'm so out of it." Troy ran his hand through his still-damp hair. "Can I just stretch out on the couch?"

Jason bit his bottom lip. "No. Take my bed. It's more comfortable."

"No way, man." Troy shook his head. "I'm imposing on you enough as it is."

"Look. It's not a problem. Take the damn bed." Jason held out his hand to Troy.

"Okay." Troy took it, and Jason pulled him to his feet.

Again that shot of awareness, triggered by Jason's touch, shot through Troy as Jason led the way to the bedroom, their hands still grasped. He let go to pull down the covers and step aside, offering the bed to Troy.

Troy sat, then slipped his legs under the covers. Jason pulled the rest over him, tucking him in as if he were a child. Troy should be pissed, but it was a kindness for which he was grateful. He snuggled down into the soft bed, his body letting go, relaxing, even as his eyes sagged shut.

"I'll check on you later." Jason's voice faded.

Troy murmured, "'Kay."

Jason stood next to the bed, staring down at the man he'd rescued. An incredible sense of protectiveness surged through him, followed closely by possessiveness and pride.

Troy needed someone, and Jason wanted to be that person. For the first time in a long time, he wanted to be there when Troy's dark eyes opened and that first sweet smile of recognition graced Troy's handsome face. The smile that would tell Jason that Troy was happy to see him, happy to be here.

Jason had never wanted to be anyone's someone. Ever. He'd always been happy to go it alone, finding company every now and then, but never really concerned about whether there would be a someone special.

Not that he didn't believe it would eventually happen.

He just never worried about it. Worrying wasn't in his nature. He believed that life happened, gave you what you needed, and you reveled in the good times and rolled with the punches.

Life had really sucker punched Troy, and Jason had a hunch Troy might need help rolling.

Jason brushed Troy's dark blond bangs from his forehead, wondering if his hair would stay dark blond or lighten as it dried. With his tanned skin, blond hair, and beach-bum name, Troy would be any gay man's fantasy.

He certainly turned Jason on. Just looking down at the sleeping man was enough to bring Jason to hard and wanting, his cock filling, tightening his jeans, making his heart pound in his chest.

He'd like nothing more than to drop to his knees and take Troy's cock in his mouth. Damn, his mouth watered at the thought of discovering Troy's taste.

As he backed away from the bed before he leaned down and kissed those perfect lips of Troy's, he knew Troy was different from all the other men who'd come in and out of his life.

Troy was what his dad used to call "a keeper."

With a keeper, you did whatever it took to hold on to that person.

Closing the door, Jason went back to the table and checked out his list of things to do to get Troy back on his feet. He scribbled down *Insurance.*

If Troy was up to it, they could start later today. Jason knew that with each thing they marked off the list, it would take Troy closer to having his life restored to him.

Closer to getting back to normal.

Closer to leaving.

"Damn." Jason closed his eyes and growled.

He didn't like it, but he figured, with a keeper like Troy, doing whatever it took to hold on to him might just mean having to let him go.

* * * * *

It was nine a.m., and Jason had to be at work by ten p.m. With the fire last night, he'd gotten no sleep at the station. His couch was too uncomfortable to sleep on, one of the reasons he'd insisted Troy take his bed.

He sat up and bit his lip, then stood, stretched out the kinks in his neck and back, and went to his bedroom.

Troy slept, curled on his side, nestled down under the blankets. With the blackout shades Jason had installed, the room was dark and cool. He needed the shades when he worked the night shift so he could sleep during the day.

Hell, the queen bed was big enough for both of them.

Jason stripped down to his briefs and crawled under the covers, taking care not to jostle Troy. For a long while, he listened to Troy's soft breathing, felt the rise and fall of his chest and the heat from his body.

He hadn't had many lovers stay over, and if they did, it was always "no strings attached." They got up in the morning, said good-bye, and went their separate ways.

Jason didn't want Troy to say good-bye. Not anytime soon.

But that was stupid. Troy would go. He'd said his friends had gone on the cruise, and when they returned, Jason was sure one of them would take Troy in.

And Jason would have to let him go.

* * * * *

Troy and Douglas had been dancing in one of the clubs, flirting shamelessly with each other. Now they were in Troy's cabin. Douglas unbuttoned Troy's shirt and raised an eyebrow. He ran his hand down Troy's chest, to the waistband of his slacks.

"You look so damn hot, Troy," Douglas told him. "Love the tan."

Troy grinned and took Douglas's mouth in a heated kiss. Douglas opened for him, and just like that, Troy knew he'd take Douglas's ass tonight.

Unzipping his trousers, he let them fall to his feet. Behind his briefs, his cock begged to be freed. Douglas hooked his fingers into the fabric and pulled them down.

Troy's dick bobbed at its liberator, its eye leaking drops of precum.

Troy moaned in anticipation. He'd waited so long for this.

Jason woke to a soft moan. Troy's body was pressed against his and Jason's free arm wrapped over Troy's waist in a loose hold. Even while he slept Jason had sought Troy out.

Troy moaned again and his hips shifted, pressing back against Jason's crotch.

That was all it took for Jason's cock to come to life, stretching, growing, stiffening against the plump ass in front of it.

Troy sighed, put his hand over Jason's hand, linked their fingers, and pulled it to his thick, long cock.

Shit. The dude's package was stellar.

Jason pushed Troy's sweats down and wrapped his hand around Troy's heated shaft.

Another moan. This time, it belonged to Jason. As Troy's hand encouraged him and his ass ground against Jason's cock, Jason dragged his hand up and down the engorged rod.

"Mmm, baby," Troy whispered, pulling his hand away, leaving Jason to jerk him off.

Jason sped up, his thumb picking up beads of precum from the head of Troy's dick, then smearing it over the shaft for lubrication. His own cock ached, but he ignored it. If there was one thing he knew, this would be for Troy. This was what he needed right now.

Release.

Troy's hips jerked as he shafted through the tight circle of Jason's hand, sliding in and out, setting Jason's cock to weeping.

Douglas jerked him off, working his dick just the way he loved it. Troy whispered, "Faster," and Douglas obeyed.

The skin on his prick superheated, the friction of palm on skin almost too exquisite to stand much longer. His balls tightened as the orgasm built inside him.

Troy's hips jerked, and he froze. Jason's hand, in a frenzy of motion, kept up the onslaught. With each pulse of his turgid flesh, Troy came, bathing Jason's hand in his cum.

Troy moaned. "Douglas," he whispered, then sighed and settled on his back in the bed.

Jason let the limp prick slip from his fingers as his stomach dropped like an elevator with its cables cut.

Who the hell was Douglas?

Troy swam up out of a deep sleep, rolled over, and opened his eyes.

Staring back at him were the bluest eyes he'd ever seen, surrounded by thick, dark lashes. For a second, he struggled to remember the face; then it hit him. Jason.

"Hi." He smiled as a wave of warmth and comfort flooded his body.

Jason's lips thinned, as if he fought smiling back. He didn't look happy.

"What's wrong? Did I sleep too late? Do you need to go to work?"

"No. I'm fine." Jason's gaze searched his.

Troy realized they were in bed. Together. Under the sheets. And Jason looked as if he was naked.

"Sorry if I chased you out of your bed." Troy grimaced.

"I told you, it's okay." Jason sounded mad, and for some reason Troy felt guilty, as if he needed to do something about it but had no idea what.

"Sure. It's okay." He nodded. He didn't know what to say, but he knew what he wanted to do. He reached out and brushed the back of his hand over Jason's cheek. A muscle twitched. "I've done something wrong, haven't I?"

Jason bit his lip, then exhaled. "Who is Douglas?"

"Douglas? How do you know about him?" Troy sat up, brushing his hair back.

Jason sat up too, pulling the covers up to his chest. "You, uh, *talk* in your sleep."

"No I don't." Troy shook his head. He never really talked. Carlton had told him once when they'd shared a room on a trip that he moaned, and he'd admitted he'd been having a sex dream.

"Technically, it was a moan," Jason informed him. "Followed by his name."

Oh shit.

Troy gasped as the fire in his face burned its way upward to his hairline.

"I'm so sorry. I don't know what to say." His hand hunted along the sheet. *Bingo.* Wet spot. Oh fuck, he'd had a wet dream and come on Jason's sheets.

"Douglas must be one hot dude." Jason's eyebrow rose as he waited for an answer.

"Well, yeah. He is." And he'd been all Troy had dreamed of for months. Why was he surprised he'd dreamed of him again last night?

"Your boyfriend?" Jason frowned.

"No." Not now. Not without the cruise. Troy frowned, remembering all his plans to make Douglas his were now charcoal briquettes.

"But you want him, right?"

Troy shrugged. "What gave me away? Besides the moaning and calling out his name."

Jason's expressive lips twisted.

"Is that why you're mad at me?" Troy wanted to touch Jason again but held back.

"Maybe it's the fact that you used *my* hand to jerk you off while you dreamed about him." Jason threw back the covers, got out of bed, and stalked out of the room.

Chapter Six

Oh this was bad.

Troy groaned, snatched a pillow off the bed, and punched it. He'd really fucked up. He should have punched himself instead of the pillow.

He got out of bed too fast, and the room spun, but he kept going in a half stagger to the living room.

Jason stood with his back to Troy, looking out of the patio window. The light from outside illuminated the front of his torso, leaving the other side in shadow as if he were carved out of marble like a Greek statue. It brought into sharp contrast the muscular build of the young man, and that he wore only black briefs.

How did Troy miss that?

"Look. Let me apologize. That was..."

"It's okay, man. You had a dream." Jason shrugged as if he didn't care, but Troy felt the heat waves of anger and hurt roll off the firefighter.

"No, it's not. I didn't even realize you'd gotten in bed with me. I was dead asleep. Dreaming."

"No, I'm sorry. I don't know why I'm so pissed." Jason turned to look Troy in the face.

"I do." Troy closed the distance between them.

"You do?" Jason searched Troy's eyes.

"There's something between us, isn't there?" Troy touched Jason on the arm where a tattooed ring of red flames circled his bicep, then trailed down until he linked their fingers. "Isn't there?"

"Yeah. I think so." Jason rolled his eyes. "I hope so. You're hot, Troy. Any man would want you in his bed."

"Just not jerking off to a dream of another man, right?" Troy snorted.

Jason laughed. "Right."

Troy slipped into Jason's personal space, right into his face. Their faces were just a lean away.

So Troy leaned.

Jason leaned, closed his eyes as their lips met...

And stole Troy's breath away with the sweetness of the kiss. It rocketed through his body, straight from his lips to his cock. Jason's tongue licked the seam of Troy's lips, and he opened, eager to accept the intrusion.

Their tongues danced that first tender dance of discovery, stroking and tasting as they listened to the soft moans of pleasure that rumbled in their chests.

Jason pulled back, then buried his hands in Troy's hair, and this time, the kiss was deep, lingering, building in intensity and need. Troy snaked his arms around Jason's neck and held on as their mouths slanted back and forth, seeking the just-right position to allow them the greatest mutual pleasure.

This was intense like Troy had never known it, not even the times with Douglas.

"Fuck." He groaned, then dived in again to get his fill of Jason's taste.

"Love to." Jason chuckled. "Now?"

"Oh yeah." Troy feathered kisses along Jason's throat.

Jason's head fell back to let him have access, and Troy nibbled and bit along the corded muscle that ran up the side of Jason's neck, to that tender spot just below his ear.

"Damn, man." Jason gasped as Troy bit him, then soothed it with a few quick licks.

"Your bed?" Troy whispered. It was official. He was king of the man whores for jumping into bed with Jason. Just a few hours ago, he'd have sworn Douglas was the man for him. Can you spell fickle? Horndog? Slut?

"Oh yeah." Jason pulled away long enough for them to make it to the bedroom, leaving any doubts Troy had in the living room. Once inside, they began to strip off Troy's clothes, which didn't take long.

Jason took Troy's already hard cock in his hand and gave it a few strokes, greeting it like an old friend. Still weak, Troy's legs trembled, and for a moment, he thought he'd collapse.

"I need to lie down." He reached behind and found the bed, then sat on the edge.

Jason pushed Troy's legs apart with his hands and fell to his knees between them, still stroking Troy's dick, making it weep.

"I have to taste you, babe." Jason bent over and took him in his mouth.

Troy fell back on the bed as Jason's hot, wet mouth captured his cock, sending shivers of delight arcing through him. He pushed a pillow under his head so he could watch.

"Shit, you're so gorgeous, Jas."

Jason pulled off his cock with a *pop.* "How did you know everyone calls me Jas?"

"Didn't. Just seemed right."

"Does when you say it." He went back to work on Troy, using the flat of his tongue to slide up and down the thick flesh, cooling it one second, then heating it in another.

Troy combed his fingers through Jason's thick, dark hair, holding him down on his cock. "That's it. Suck me." He kept his gaze on the sight of Jason's head bobbing up and down, swallowing his dick. It was so fucking hot, he thought he'd come if he kept staring at it.

Jason released him and attacked Troy's balls. In preparation for the trip, he'd had them waxed. God, he loved having them sucked, and Jason knew how to do it, pulling them inside his mouth, working his tongue over the hard nut inside, then pulling, letting go, pulling, letting go, until Troy writhed on the bed in a dance of agony and ecstasy.

"You need a cock ring. I'd love to see your balls wrapped in a leather band." Jason sat back and admired Troy's dick. He bounced it against his tongue, then wiggled the tip of his tongue into the small red slit in the plump head.

Troy laughed. "Bit of a Dom, huh?"

"Yeah. You with a leather thong around your neck to match the cock ring would be so hot, babe."

"Like a collar?" Troy's eyes widened. He'd never played like that before, and it sent a rush of excitement like an arrow to his balls. It sounded wicked. Over the edge.

"You like that idea? Wearing my collar?"

For some reason, he did. Troy licked his lips. "What would it mean, exactly?"

Jason licked up Troy's dick, making him shiver. "That you belong to me. Just for the next week," he added quickly.

"Belong? Like a slave?" Troy grimaced. He didn't like the sound of that.

"No. Like you've given me the ultimate gift—your body. That you trust me enough to take you as far as you can go safely to obtain maximum pleasure."

Troy swallowed. He'd heard of subs and Doms; who hadn't? But hearing about it and doing it were two different things. He wasn't the sub type. He'd always been the one in charge, and he'd topped most of the time, but he wasn't against bottoming. With the right guy, it was grade-A choice. But the right guys had been few and far between.

He'd thought Douglas was the right guy, had let him take his ass. And it was good, but something had been missing. But this, right now, blew him away.

"If it means you're going to beat me, forget it." Troy didn't think his body could stand any more pain. Not after the fire.

Jason must have read the fear in his eyes. "No, man. I'd never hurt you. I'm not into causing pain, just pleasure. I'm into bondage. Bindings." He continued to jerk Troy off, his hand twisting and pumping.

"I've never been that adventurous, you know." Troy laughed.

"Well, I'm all about adventure, babe." Jason grinned.

"What if I don't like it?"

"We quit." Jason licked his balls, his blue gaze focused on Troy's.

"Just like that?"

"Yeah. Just like that. I won't do anything you don't want me to do, or keep doing anything that hurts. Okay?" Jason searched Troy's face.

It was only for the next week. It would be different from anything he'd done before, and right now, Troy wanted different, wanted to be wild, wanted to feel alive.

"Okay." Troy exhaled. "When do we start?"

"Right now, if you're ready." Jason sat back on his heels.

"What do you want to do to me?" Troy whispered.

"You like it, huh?" Jason held Troy's cock upright. "See, stiff as a rod. It knows what it wants, Troy."

"I guess so."

"I'm going to bind you." He dipped down and took Troy's cock to the root and sucked hard.

Troy tensed. "Bind me? Where? With what?"

"Your cock and balls. I'm going to use a silk tie."

Oh shit. He'd been turned on last night when Carlton had suggested tying Douglas down to keep him in his room, but this burst of arousal exceeded that one. On the Richter sex scale, it was a seven-point *Oh Oh Oh God*. He took a deep breath.

"Do it." He exhaled and gave himself to Jason.

Chapter Seven

Troy stretched out on the bed, stroking himself as Jason went to his dresser and searched through it.

"Here's what I need." Jason turned around, holding up a long brown silk tie.

Swallowing down a lump, Troy nodded. Just the sight of the restraint sent a shot of arousal to his dick.

Jason crawled onto the bed next to him. He draped the tie over Troy's chest and pulled it across. The silk fabric glided over his skin, and Troy shivered. Jason moved it as if it were a snake, back and forth, up and down, closer and closer to Troy's straining dick.

When the tie touched the head of his cock, Troy thought he'd lose it. Just shoot his load.

Somehow, he held on, not willing to miss what Jason had planned for him.

Jason ran his hand over Troy's body in the tie's wake, the rough skin of his hand a sharp contrast to the smooth texture of the silk. Troy shuddered.

"You're so gorgeous. Do you know how much your body turns me on?" Jason whispered.

"Does it?" Troy ran a hand over his stomach up to his nipple and played with it as he continued to pump his thick cock.

"Fuck yes." Jason ran the tie over the underside of Troy's dick, and they both shuddered.

Jason looked up, caught Troy's eye, and they smiled at each other.

"Now, for the binding." Jason grinned; then his gaze focused on Troy's cock.

"For now, this is mine." Jason pushed Troy's hand away, leaving the erection to flop against Troy's thigh. "So pretty." He ran the tie over it again. "Let me do everything."

He raised Troy's leg, bent it at the knee, and wrapped one end of the tie around Troy's thigh, strapping his cock to it.

"Too tight?" he asked.

Troy shook his head.

Jason tightened the binding until Troy sucked in his breath. He tied the first knot.

"Now?" Jason's wicked smile turned Troy on even more than seeing his dick strapped to his leg.

"Yes."

"Good."

Jason brought the rest of the tie up and over, then threaded it under Troy's balls. Troy's sac pulled tight as his balls drew up under the touch of the silk as it slid along the delicate skin.

Troy watched as Jason took his time wrapping the silk tie around them, pulling it tight, and tying the second knot. They bulged, the skin completely tight, exposing his pink nuts to Jason. His cock strained against the restraint in response.

Even his nipples strained for relief. Troy applied a few tweaks to the one he played with, sending tiny shocks through his body.

Christ, he was going to lose it and come.

"Don't come, babe. Hold off."

"Can't," Troy gasped.

Jason nodded. He pulled the bindings tighter around Troy's cock and balls, creating an on-the-fly cock-and-balls ring, cutting off Troy's orgasm.

"Shit!" Troy groaned.

"Now, you're mine. I control you. I control what I do to you. I control when you'll come. Do you understand?" Jason's pupils grew wide and his irises changed to a deeper shade of blue in his arousal.

"Yes." Troy nodded. God, he was so turned on. And eager to see what Jason would do to him and how far Jason would take him before he begged to be released from his bindings.

The idea of begging sent another blast of arousal straight to his dick, and he moaned with the pleasure and the sweet pain of it.

Jason continued wrapping the end of the long tie over Troy's other thigh, then back to tie it off with an elaborate knot. The pattern of it against his skin was like a piece of art.

"Learn that in Boy Scouts?" Troy choked out. There was beauty in the precise knot.

"Something like that." Jason ran his hand over Troy's thigh.

"I never was a Boy Scout." Troy chuckled.

"Neither was I. Just liked knots." Jason pulled on the trailing line of silk. Somehow, it tightened on his dick. Troy had no idea how Jason had managed that trick, but at this point he no longer cared.

Precum oozed out and dripped onto his thigh, leaving more evidence of how turned on he was.

Jason moaned. "Goddamn, it's so beautiful. The way the tie crosses your skin, the brown silk against the color of your skin. That's one beautiful tan, Troy. It's perfect."

"Thanks, I guess." Troy hissed as Jason pulled again and the knot tightened around his balls.

Jason leaned over and licked a line down the side of Troy's cock to the even-thicker head. Troy cried out, his back arching at the unexpected sensitivity of warm tongue on throbbing, heated flesh.

Jason played his tongue over the plump head, lapping up the line of precum as it dripped down the inside of Troy's thigh. Troy spread his legs wider to accommodate Jason.

It was torture, but Troy wanted it to continue until he couldn't take one more touch, one more kiss, one more lick on his hypersensitive dick.

Jason licked Troy's balls, the heat of his tongue burning the sensitive, taut skin. He gasped as Jason engulfed both nuts in his mouth and sucked them.

"Oh shit, Jas!" His back arched, and he pinched his nipple.

The sucking brought tears to Troy's eyes, but he couldn't end it now. He wanted to go all the way, and he wasn't there yet. Just like on the ledge of his building, he'd hang on for as long as possible.

Jason let Troy's nuts go and then licked Troy's cock, taking slow, long passes over it, from the base to the dripping tip. Jason angled his head and took the swollen red cap into his mouth. His tongue invaded the slit, and Troy cried out again.

"Is that a stop?"

Troy's body ached to come, his balls burned, full of his seed, ready to unload, and his cock strained against the bindings, thick and hard. If it had been loose, it would have stood straight up against his belly like a steel rod.

He wanted, needed, to come.

"No!" Troy took a deep breath and held it. "No," he said again, this time softer as he gained control. "Not yet."

"More?" Jason smiled. "That's my man."

He got off the bed, leaving Troy alone, then went back to the dresser. He returned with a thin piece of black leather, letting it play between his fingers as he ran it across his palm.

"What are you going to do with that?" Troy's heartbeat pounded, a heavy drumbeat echo to the blood thumping in his captured dick.

"This is for your throat." Jason got on the bed and moved to Troy's shoulders. He slipped the leather cord under Troy's neck.

Troy swallowed, his body tensed, and for a moment, terror shot through him. It must have shown in his eyes.

"No, babe, no. I'm not going to hurt you." Jason frowned, his own eyes looking hurt, as if Troy's just thinking it pained him as he brushed Troy's bangs from his forehead.

Troy relaxed and nodded.

Jason sighed, then leaned down to kiss him. As his lips feathered over Troy's in a whisper of a touch, Troy felt tenderness, and if he hadn't been so on the edge, he'd have sworn the kiss had held love. But that was too much, too fast, too soon. He had to be losing his mind to even think that Jason would care for him that way.

After all, this was just about sex, wasn't it?

Jason's erection strained against his belly as he'd slipped the leather thong around Troy's neck. Jason wore it when he went out to the clubs, looking for a similar soul to play with. He'd met a few men before, but no one as responsive, as open, as gorgeous, as Troy.

He brought the ends around to tie the knot.

A knot that would have to be cut to be released.

"Once I tie this, it will have to be cut off." Jason stared into Troy's eyes, willing him to understand what this meant to him. To them.

Troy blinked and searched Jason's eyes. Then he smiled.

"Oh."

"Oh, what?" Jason's hopes rose along with his balls.

"This means I'm yours. As long as I wear it, right?"

"Yes." Jason bit his bottom lip and nodded, hoping foolish hopes. Time seemed to stop as he waited for Troy's decision. His cock ached to be inside this man, his ass ached to be filled by him. If he refused, Jason knew he'd be shattered by it, and that scared him almost as much as the rejection.

"Tie it, Jason," Troy whispered and raised his chin to give Jason more access.

Jason almost came. His hands shook as he tied the knot. Then he jumped off the bed and went to the bathroom, getting a glass of water before returning to the bed.

"What's the water for?"

"The knot." He tipped the glass over, trickling a thin line of water over the leather knot. "As it dries, it will tighten. Not the cord around your neck, just the knot."

Troy shivered as the water dripped down his neck and over his shoulder.

Jason put the glass on the nightstand, then kissed Troy, his lips soft and full. He traced his tongue along Troy's seam, and Troy groaned and opened for him. Slipping inside, Jason tasted his lover. His lover. God he loved that way that sounded.

That odd feeling of possessiveness and pride ripped through him again.

Troy looked down at Jason's erection, hunger burning in his gaze. Jason had leaked precum all over his belly as he'd worked with the leather thong. Troy reached out his hand and ran his fingers through the smears.

Bringing it to his mouth, he sucked his fingers in and moaned, nearly setting off Jason.

He pulled on his balls, their need to empty burning in him.

Troy licked each finger, then sighed. "I want more. Want you to come in my mouth."

"Oh God. Oh shit." Kneeling, Jason straddled Troy's shoulders, spreading his legs wider to accommodate their width.

Troy's mouth opened, and Jason thrust in.

"Ahhh," Jason cried out as incredible warmth enveloped his dick.

Troy began to suck him off, strong, hard pulls, hollowing his cheeks with the effort. Jason stared down at the most beautiful sight he'd ever seen.

Troy's full lips wrapped around his cock, his cock sliding in and out as he pumped. Troy's hand came up and twisted around the base, jerking him off as he sucked him off.

Unable to stay upright, Jason put his hands out and leaned against the wall as his hips thrust, fucking Troy's glorious mouth.

"Take it, babe. Suck me." Jason growled, thrusting harder.

Troy's answering pull nearly did it for Jason.

He held on, fighting against the need to come and spill down Troy's throat.

Troy stuck a finger along Jason's cock, wetting it in his mouth.

As Jason hammered him, Troy ran his wet finger from Jason's balls to his puckered hole, pushed in, breaching Jason's ass, and hit his gland.

Jason screamed and came, pumping hot and hard into Troy.

Troy swallowed, massaging Jason's cock even as it emptied.

Head down, Jason rested all his weight against the wall to hold himself up as he shuddered through the last of his orgasm.

Troy let go, and Jason's softening prick slipped free.

"Goddamn, Jas." Troy groaned. "That was so fucking hot."

Jason swung one leg over and scooted down on the bed next to Troy, gathering him in his arms.

"You have no idea." He nuzzled Troy's neck.

"Sure I do." Troy jerked his shoulder. "Did you forget something?"

Jason looked up. "Shit!" He sat up and reached for the bindings.

"Not so fast, lover." Troy smiled. "I want you to finish what you started."

Jason couldn't keep his grin from breaking across his face.

Chapter Eight

He was the luckiest son of a bitch in the world. He'd found Troy, and Troy was more than willing to experiment. Jason's cock stirred just thinking about what he wanted to do with him.

Troy's cock and balls were still bound tight to his thigh, and incredibly, his dick was still hard. He must have been hurting, tied up for so long.

"Should I loosen the bindings?" Jason ran a finger between the tie wrapped around Troy's thigh.

"No. I'm fine. I just need to come, that's all." Troy groaned.

"Not to worry, babe. I'll let you come." Jason moved his finger along the tie until it reached Troy's cock. "God, I love how this looks. Your dick all tied up, straining to stand up."

"I know it sounds weird, but it really turns me on to be tied up like this. Sick, huh?" Troy looked into Jason's eyes for an answer.

"No, it's not sick. It's erotic. It's a fucking turn-on. Anyone would get hard seeing this. Having you bound like this." Jason leaned over Troy and kissed him.

Troy sighed. "Good. I was beginning to think I was strange."

"Look, the way I see it is this." He ran his hand over Troy's shaft as he nibbled on his neck. "If it turns me on and turns you on and no one is getting hurt, what's the big deal?"

"That's one way to look at it, I guess." Troy groaned. "Now. About my problem?"

"Problem?" Jason nipped his way down Troy's body, giving each nipple a bite, a lick, and then a hard suck.

Troy pressed Jason's head down and held him there; his body arched as he tried to push his nipple farther into Jason's mouth. Jason worked the hard nub with his teeth, pulling at it, loving how his lover responded to his touch.

"Nipple rings. You need a pair." Jason growled.

"Only if you get a pair too." Troy laughed. "I'm not going to be the only one of us who that gets holes put in his nips."

"Okay." Jason nodded. "Silver for me, gold for you."

Troy watched as Jason licked his way to Troy's navel, circled it, and then plunged in. His tongue wiggled, tickling him. In his heightened state, even being tickled turned him on.

"Like that?" Jason asked.

"Yeah, it feels good. You playing with me." Troy stroked his hand through Jason's dark hair. "More."

"More, huh?" Jason ran his tongue over Troy's hip, then angled off toward the crease where hip met thigh and Troy's cock had been tied down.

Jason let his tongue dance over the heated flesh of Troy's erection and felt it jerk.

"It likes."

Troy nodded. "It would like it even more if it could just fucking come."

Jason untied the first knot and pulled the tie away from Troy's body. He unwrapped it, letting the silk slide over Troy's skin. Troy closed his eyes, focusing on the sensation of silk, Jason's fingers, and the way Jason kissed and nipped at his body.

Another knot came undone, and with it his cock found freedom.

It rose as if resurrected from the grave, a stiff spike. Sparks of arousal shot up and down his cock as it landed against his belly, and Troy groaned. Only his balls were bound now and that was the only thing keeping him from shooting his load.

"My balls. Untie them."

"Not yet." Jason spit, took Troy's dick in his hand, and pumped it. He lowered his mouth over the plump, dripping head.

Troy moaned as Jason worked him over, leaving no sexual stone unturned. Licking, biting, sucking, Jason used teeth, tongue, lips, and even at one point, his stubbled cheek, to send a string of unending sensations straight to Troy's balls.

They tightened and burned with the building need to unload. It was torment. It was pleasure like he'd never known it. He hung on the edge of release for what seemed like forever.

Troy buried both hands in Jason's hair and pulled, then begged, "Please, let me come!"

Jason released Troy's balls.

Troy's orgasm ripped through him, a dam finally giving way under the intense pressure, and he pumped his hips, fucking Jason's mouth, giving him every drop of cum he had in his body.

"Oh God. So fucking good," he gasped, then fell back to bed, spent and boneless.

Jason licked him clean, tossed the tie on the floor, and then crawled up to snuggle with Troy. He buried his face in the crook of Troy's neck and shoulder and gave him a kiss.

"Sleep. I need sleep."

Troy snorted. "You're one of those guys, huh?" He ran his hand through Jason's hair, petting him while his other hand held Jason tight to him.

"Yes, I am," said a muffled voice.

"Good. So am I."

Happy, spent, and exhausted beyond anything he'd known, Troy held his lover and closed his eyes.

So what if it wasn't his dream vacation?

So what if this wasn't Douglas?

Chapter Nine

"**H**ey, wake up." Jason shook Troy's shoulder.

Troy rolled over and yawned. "Is it morning?"

"No, man. It's a little after one in the afternoon. I think, if we pull ourselves together, we can get over to the DPS office and get your driver's license replaced."

"You think so?" Troy sat up and scratched his chest. His hand wandered to the thong around his neck, and he played with the knot. Instead of tight and constraining, it felt safe, as if it protected him like a talisman.

Jason leaned over and kissed his cheek. "Yeah. On our way, you can call your insurance agent. You had insurance, didn't you?"

"Yes, thank God. Renters. And car, of course. Good idea."

Jason got out of bed, tossed the clothes Troy had been wearing at him, and got dressed. "How about some burgers at the drive-through?"

"Sounds great. I'm starved." Troy slipped into the sweats and T-shirt, but looked up at Jason and frowned. "No shoes."

Jason went to the closet. "Here, try these on." He tossed a pair of running shoes at Troy, then went to his dresser and pulled open a drawer. "Socks." A white bundle flew over Troy's head, and Troy snagged it out of the air.

"Slow down, man." Troy laughed as he pulled on the socks. "Hey, the shoes fit."

"Told you we're about the same size." Jason grinned, then slapped his hands together. "Let's go. There's no telling how long the DPS will take."

"Right." Troy stood, groaned as his aching muscles protested, then hurried after Jason.

After a quick call to his insurance agent using Jason's trendy iPhone, Troy felt better. They swung by the agent's office, where a check waited for Troy with an advance on some living expenses through his policy.

His agent even printed out new insurance cards for him and gave him the name and number of the dealership so he could get a new set of car keys.

They left there and headed to the DPS.

After a two-hour wait in a snaking, creeping line, they made it to the counter and a clerk, explained the situation, handed over the papers from the insurance agent, and within fifteen minutes, Troy had his driver's license in hand.

"So far, so good." Jason chuckled.

"Bank next. I want to cash this check and get my credit and debit cards replaced." Troy relaxed into the seat of the Explorer as Jason drove. "What time do you go to work?"

"I'm on the ten-to-six shift this week. I have Friday night off."

"I can't tell you how much this means to me, man. If it weren't for you, I don't know where I'd be or how I'd be able to do any of this. Everyone I know is out of town." Troy frowned and turned away, not wanting to let Jason see the wet gathering in his eyes.

"Don't mention it. Really. Don't say another word. For what it's worth, I'd do it again." Jason reached out and squeezed

Troy's hand. Troy covered it with his own and nodded.

"I need some clothes. Can we hit a store before you go to work? Just to get a few things?"

"Like underwear? Or do you usually go commando?" Jason winked.

"Briefs, actually." Troy sniffed. "The boys like their support."

Jason laughed. "I know. After years of wearing a cup for sports, once I graduated and stop playing it felt weird not having one on."

"Yeah, you get used to it."

They talked about the sports they'd played as Jason drove to Troy's bank. Small talk, like his family, his work, and his interests, once so forced, came easy between Troy and Jason.

All this was easy. Because of Jason. His rescuer.

Troy had no idea if this was some survivor thing, but life seemed sweeter, more tangible, as if he could reach out and touch it, hold it in his hand. Hold it to his heart.

By five o'clock, Troy had money in his hand, and a new credit/debit card would be waiting for him at the bank in the morning. They'd made real progress, and with each piece of his life they recovered, the stress and tension in his body and mind eased.

A lot of it had to do with being around Jason. The man had a puppylike exuberance Troy had rarely seen. Jason not only looked a few years younger, his attitude was so much fresher, so less jaded and cynical than Troy's other friends, including Douglas.

Troy grunted. That was the first time all day he'd thought of Douglas.

"What's up?" Jason raised an eyebrow.

"Nothing. Just thinking."

"About?"

Troy sighed. "Dinner. I'm starved. That burger and soda wasn't enough. I could eat a horse."

"Well, if it's meat you want, then you'll be wanting barbecue, right?"

Troy laughed. "Well, if it's from Goode's, you got that right!"

"I think we've done enough for today, babe. Let's get dinner and go home."

"You need to get some sleep, don't you?" Troy ran his hand over Jason's thigh. He'd taken all Jason's time. "I bet you sleep most of the day and I've screwed up your schedule."

"Not really. I usually sleep for a few hours after and before my shift, so if we eat quick, I can still catch a few hours." Jason shrugged.

"Good. Last thing I want to do is to make things hard for you. You've been unbelievable. Just fucking incredible. I really owe you." Troy ran his hand over his face. "You saved my life, you know. I owe you." Tears burned in his eyes. "Sorry, Jas, I don't know what the hell is wrong with me. I'm usually not so emo."

"Hey, don't apologize to me. You almost died last night. You have every right to be a little on the edge. I understand."

Those words seemed to ease Troy, and he took a deep breath, held it, and then let it out slow. "Thanks."

"And just for the record, Troy. You don't owe me a damn thing. Got it? I don't want you doing anything because you feel you have to, to pay me back. Okay?" Jason looked into Troy's eyes, and Troy felt the pull all the way to his balls.

"Okay." Troy nodded.

They drove for a while in silence.

"You haven't, have you?" Jason asked as his teeth worried his bottom lip.

"Haven't what?"

"The things we've done together. You didn't do them because you felt like you owed it to me, right?"

"No. I'm doing them because I want to." Troy put his hand on Jason's thigh and gave it a squeeze.

"Good." Jason's body seemed to relax, and Troy realized how tense he'd been.

They pulled up at a department store. "Is this okay?" Jason asked. It was one Troy had shopped at before, and he liked their selection.

"Perfect." Troy got out and followed Jason inside.

Troy went to his usual section of men's clothing, but Jason took one look at the racks of Dockers and polo shirts and made a face that looked as if he smelled a dead skunk.

"You're kidding me, right?" He leaned on the rack Troy was going through.

"What's wrong with these?"

"Boring," Jason sang out. He grabbed Troy's hand and dragged him across the aisle to the young men's section, filled with casual shorts, colorful shirts, and faded jeans.

Jason pulled out a shirt and held it out. "This would look great on you."

"You think?" Troy took the shirt and held it up to him. It was definitely not his style, but he couldn't deny he was attracted to the bright colors and prints.

"Yeah." Jason rolled his eyes.

The clothes would have been great on his cruise.

Troy frowned. What were his pals doing now? They'd planned to hike to Dunn Falls in the Cayman's and visit a rum factory. Party all night. Snorkel among the reefs. Instead, he was left here, trying to put his life back in order.

Some vacation.

Jason moved on, pulling out shirts, jeans, and shorts, and passing them to Troy. "Let's go try them on." Troy followed the younger man to the dressing room, both of their arms draped with clothes.

A salesman approached them. "Need help?"

"No, man. He's just going to try these on." Jason pushed Troy toward a dressing room and then helped him hang up all the clothes. As Jason pulled the door shut, he gave Troy a sexy wink. "Come out here when you've got that shirt and those jeans on and give me a show."

Troy had only meant to grab a few things, but here he was surrounded by dozens of items, ready to model them for Jason. He slipped into the clothes Jason had pointed out and left the small room.

Standing in front of the three-way mirror, he asked, "What do you think?"

"You look hot, man." Jason nodded from his seat in a chair.

Troy stared at his reflection. The worn jeans hung low on his narrow hips and the white shirt with red flames around the bottom that Jason had picked out for him set off his dark tan, blond hair, and brown eyes. It wasn't his usual style, but he had to admit, he looked good. And younger.

How the hell did clothes take a few years off him?

He stared at his face. He smiled back.

Behind Troy in the mirror, Jason grinned at him, lust in his eyes.

Oh yeah, he felt younger. Sexier. Damn it, he *was* hot.

Jason stood, grabbed Troy's hand, and rushed to the door of the small dressing room Troy had used. "Get inside. Now," he said in a hoarse whisper.

Troy frowned. "Is there something else you'd like to see me try on?"

"Yeah. Let's try my mouth on your dick," Jason whispered. He pulled Troy inside the room and shut the door. A wave of arousal swept over Troy as Jason slipped the flimsy sliding bolt closed.

"There are people outside," Troy whispered back. He didn't want to admit how turned on he was, how little frissons of excitement danced up and down his spine and stiffened his cock. "We could get caught."

"I know. How hot is that?" Jason fell to his knees, undoing the button and zipper on the jeans, and then pulled them down around Troy's hips. Troy's dick sprung free.

Jason took Troy's cock in his mouth and sucked. Troy had to stifle a moan, afraid someone would hear them. Christ, would they call security? The cops? Would this be on the news? *Two gay men arrested for engaging in sex at local department store.*

That idea just made it seem even hotter. This was so not like him. It must be the near-death experience that had him acting so reckless and out of character.

Jason's hand supported him against the wall, while his other hand played with Troy's balls. Troy leaned back against the wall of the booth and watched their reflection in the mirror. Goddamn, it was so fucking hot to see Jason going down on him, his dark head as it moved back and forth, and the expanse of his own brown cock appearing and disappearing in Jason's mouth.

"Can I help you find anything else?" The salesman's voice floated over the door of the room.

Chapter Ten

S*hit*. Troy squeezed his fist in Jason's hair, ready to pull him off, but Jason let him go. "No, thanks. We've got it in hand." He winked up at Troy, and Troy nearly lost it, biting his lip to keep from laughing.

"Okay. Let me know if you do." The man moved away. Troy was positive the guy knew what they were doing, and that made it even hotter.

Jason glanced up at him, grinned, and then swallowed Troy's dick to the root.

Troy's head flew back, hitting the wall of the enclosure with a hard *thud.*

"Ow!"

"Are you all right?" Damn, wouldn't the salesman go away?

"Fine," Troy squeaked out as Jason sucked one of his balls inside his warm, wet mouth, swirling his tongue around it until Troy thought he'd scream.

"If you're sure." The guy chuckled.

"Positive," Troy croaked.

He looked down at Jason. Jason wiggled his eyebrows and went back to sucking him off. His gaze shot from Jason's reflection in the mirror to Jason's mouth and back again, each one more erotic than the next, building the tension in his balls to a delicious high.

"Gonna come," Troy whispered.

"Mm-mmm," Jason hummed.

The soft vibration and Jason's tongue manipulating the bundle of nerves under the head of his cock sent Troy over the edge.

He shot his load down Jason's throat as he whimpered.

Jason licked him clean, put him back in his jeans, and zipped up as Troy's legs gave out and he sat on the tiny shelf of a seat in the corner of the dressing room.

"Oh God." He ran his hand over his face and looked at Jason, who was unzipping his jeans. He pulled out his cock. It was stiff and red and looked wickedly delicious.

"Your turn," Jason whispered, holding his dick out.

Jason stood in front of Troy as he sat on the ledge and swallowed down Jason's thick cock. The velvety skin slid easily into his mouth, the cap hitting the back of his throat, causing his spent cock to twitch. In only a short time, Troy already loved the taste of him, the scent that belonged only to the man who'd rescued him and taken him in.

Jason reached down and looped a finger under the leather strap around Troy's neck.

"Damn, you look so hot in this." His eyes narrowed as he sucked in a breath.

Troy looked into the mirror. He loved the way Jason looked at him, with a deep possessiveness he'd never seen in any man's eyes. Wrapping his hand around the base of Jason's shaft, he twisted and stroked it as he sucked like a kid with a Popsicle.

Jason wrapped one hand in Troy's hair, stared into his eyes, and the connection between them shot straight to his heart. Now that was a turn-on he hadn't felt in ages.

"That's it, babe. Suck me." Troy feared Jason's low voice carried over the top of the flimsy door, but he was so aroused, he didn't care. He renewed his attack as he watched his reflection give Jason a blowjob.

Troy wet his finger in his mouth, resumed blowing Jason, and ran his damp digit under Jason's balls and straight to his hole. He slipped it in, and Jason gasped.

"Oh fuck!"

A snicker came from the other side of the door. The damn salesman was listening to them. Jason met Troy's gaze as both of them struggled to keep from laughing.

Jason winked at him and let out a loud moan, and Troy smiled around the thick shaft in his mouth.

There was a gasp and a thud from the other side of the door.

Jason reached over and slid the lock open. "Come in, if you want."

Troy's stomach plummeted. He couldn't believe Jason had invited the other man in while he was giving him a blowjob. He couldn't believe how hard that made him either.

The door opened, and the older man slid inside. Eyes wide open, mouth matching, he locked the door behind him and leaned against the opposite wall.

Oh fuck. Why the hell not? Troy began bobbing up and down on Jason's dick.

The salesman rubbed his hand over his dress slacks and the noticeable erection he sported.

Jason whispered, "Do it, man."

The man unzipped and pulled out his dick. It wasn't as big as Troy's or Jason's, but it was thick. He spit into his hand and worked it as he watched the two men. He spread his legs and leaned against the wall, jerking off.

"Over here," Jason commanded.

The man moved to his side, and Jason reached out and covered the guy's hand as he stroked. The man moaned, his eyes shuttering, as Jason took over.

Troy's own cock stiffened again, and using one hand he got his jeans open and his dick out. At his level, he watched Jason jerking off the other man and Troy's cock throbbed in his hand as he stroked it, smearing precum from the tip over the shaft.

Now all three men were getting off, Troy sitting on the bench, doing himself and blowing Jason, Jason standing, jerking off the salesman, and the salesman leaning against the wall for support.

The air in the small dressing room was thick with sex, sweat, and soft moans. It went straight to Troy's head, as intoxicating as straight shots of tequila. He'd never done anything like this before.

Troy wondered who'd blow first.

Jason pulled Troy off his cock, then leaned down and took Jason's mouth in a hard, possessive kiss. Troy opened for him, and their tongues dueled.

As the salesman watched them, he groaned and shot all over the wall of the room, head back, eyes closed, and shuddering. Jason pulled Troy off the bench and held their cocks together as Troy jerked them off with both hands. Together, they came, shooting cum all over the new shirt Troy had been modeling.

"Fucking fantastic!" Jason leaned back, panting. It was all Troy could do to nod.

The salesman swallowed, looked at them, frowned, and said, "You'll have to pay for the shirt, guys."

Jason and Troy leaned together, arms wrapped around each other, and laughed.

It took Troy, Jason, and the sales guy to carry all the clothes to the register.

"New wardrobe?" he asked as he rang up the merchandise.

"My apartment burned. Everything's gone." Troy shrugged. He didn't want to say more. It'd just remind him, and he'd get all depressed and ruin his good mood.

"That sucks." The guy paused and looked around. "Look, I can give you a twenty percent discount on this."

Troy smiled. "God, thanks. That's really nice of you."

"No," he said, leaning forward. "It was really nice of you. Both of you." He gave them a wink.

Jason slung his arm around Troy and laughed. "For all of us, man."

Next to the register was a stand with an assortment of leather wallets and belts. Troy looked it over and chose a wallet and two belts, then added it to the pile of clothes.

As the salesman bagged it all up, Troy pulled out his cash and paid for it. Then Troy and Jason went to the car and loaded it all in the back.

"You were awesome, Troy. I didn't think you'd go for that at first." Jason leaned over and bit Troy's ear, sending a jolt of desire through Troy. His dick filled and he shifted in the seat of the car, trying to ease his growing erection.

"Neither did I. It was wild, exciting, but risky as hell. I've never done anything like that before."

"Stick with me and you'll be hooked on the rush." Jason grinned at him. Troy didn't know about the rush, but hooked on Jason? Oh yeah, he could see that.

"If you keep that up, there won't be any rest for the wicked," Troy warned.

"I've worked on less sleep, believe me."

"Maybe, but I'd never forgive myself if anything happened to you because of me. I'm serious, Jas. When we get home, you go straight to bed."

"I like it when you're demanding, babe." Jason wiggled his eyebrows at Troy. "Turns me on." Jason slid his hand up Troy's thigh. God, the man was insatiable. Troy liked that, a lot.

"Yeah, well, forget it. We can get together in the morning." Laughing, Troy pushed Jason's hand away.

"Morning sex. That's the best. I love it after I come off duty."

"I'll bet you do. All smelly and sweaty and musky." Troy shivered at the thought of Jason stretched out on the bed and how Troy would take his time tasting the man with his tongue.

Jason raised his arm, offering his pit. "Here. Take a whiff. See what you're missing."

Troy laughed and punched Jason in the ribs. "Jerk. I'm *not* smelling your armpit."

"You know you want it, dude."

"No, I don't." Troy looked out the window and folded his arms across his chest.

"Yeah, you do." Jason's smug grin made him laugh; he couldn't help it.

Damn, but Jason was so much fun to be around. Here Troy was, everything he owned gone, trying to get some normal back in his life, and he was having sex in dressing rooms, joking around, and feeling better than he'd felt in a long time.

"Yeah, I do," Troy confessed.

Jason's laugh filled the cabin of the SUV as his shoulders shook and Troy joined in, laughing until his eyes leaked tears.

"Stop it. I'm going to piss myself." Troy held his stomach as he tried to control his laughter.

Jason swatted Troy's belly with the back of his hand. "Don't ruin the seats, man. Just had the car cleaned."

That just sent Troy off again.

Jason leaned over and turned on the radio. "Cool. I love this song." He began to sing along.

It was one Troy knew and liked also.

They sang all the way to the restaurant.

Chapter Eleven

Troy dumped his bags on the couch and sat next to them. "Get some rest and don't worry about me. I'll just watch TV until you go to work. I don't want to throw you out of your routine."

"You're not. And it's okay. Usually, I get some sleep at the station. After we do our equipment checks, some of us turn in. If there're no calls, we sleep all night."

"Does that happen often?" Troy asked.

"Sometimes. But our station gets alarms for several others in the area, so the bell goes off all the time. You just get used to it."

"Wow. How do you know which bell is for your station?"

"Different tones. You learn real quick which one is yours." Jason grinned. "Okay.

I'm going to take a nap. Sure you won't join me?" He winked.

"If I did, you wouldn't sleep." Troy tossed a throw pillow at Jason, who caught it.

"Damn straight." Jason tossed it back and loped over to the kitchen. He took a bottle of juice from the fridge and downed it. Troy enjoyed watching the younger man. Everything about him was sexy, and there was nothing Troy would like better than to crawl into bed with him. Bad idea. Jason should get some rest.

After tossing the plastic bottle in the garbage, Jason loped back to Troy, leaned down, and kissed him. Troy opened for him without being asked. Their tongues wrangled; then Jason broke the kiss.

"Better get to bed."

"Do I need to wake you up?"

"No, man. My alarm's set. See you around nine thirty." With that, he slipped into his bedroom and shut the door.

Troy sat back on the couch, staring at the door. The room seemed to have lost some of its life when Jason left. Troy seemed to have lost something too. Could be, Jason's excitement was infectious. Could be, the younger man was getting to him.

Could be, when Jason was around, Troy just felt better. Happier.

He picked up the remote control, turned the sound down, and checked out what was on TV.

* * * * *

Jason stood with his shoes in his hand and looked down at Troy. The man he'd rescued and taken into his home had stretched out on the floor, his back against the couch, and fallen asleep.

He looked good. Jason couldn't believe how lucky he was. Troy was so incredibly handsome. And that tan? The blond hair? Man, that just made him nuts.

"Troy?" Jason squatted down and shook Troy's shoulder.

"Jas?" Troy jerked awake. "Time to go?"

"Yeah. I gotta go." Jason stood, dropped his shoes to the floor, then sat on the couch to put them on.

Troy stretched, stood, and picked up the bags from the department store. "Can I pile these up somewhere?"

"Use my room. I cleaned out a drawer for you, and there are some hangers in the closet. Just put your stuff away, okay?" Jason pulled the strings on his sneakers tight and stood. "Shift's over at six. I'll be back before seven."

"Okay. Wake me up when you get home." Troy stood there, the bags still clutched in his hands, looking unsure what he should do.

Jason sure as hell knew what he wanted. He took the bags from Troy, tossed them back on the sofa, then grabbed Troy by the shoulders and pulled him into a bear hug.

At first, Troy didn't move. Then he sighed, slipped his arms around Jason's waist, laid his head on Jason's shoulder, and melted into the embrace.

Jason squeezed him tighter, then let him go. "You're going to be fine, man. Really. It's all going to be okay." He brushed a lock of hair from Troy's forehead.

Troy nodded. "I know."

"Give me a kiss, then."

Troy took Jason's mouth hard. A bit of desperation. A bit of lust. Jason liked that combination. His dick twitched in his jeans, and he reached down to adjust himself.

"Damn. You do it to me." Jason grinned.

God, Jason drove Troy wild. He was so out there. So open with what he felt, what he wanted. And it was deliciously clear he wanted Troy.

Troy laughed. "I'll see you in the morning. Take care of yourself."

Jason headed to the door. "See you." With another of his flirty winks, he was out the door and gone.

Troy picked up the bags and carried them to the bedroom. He tossed them on the bed and pulled everything out. Then he opened the top drawer. Just as Jason had said, the drawer had been cleared. Troy put his new underwear and socks in and slid it shut.

At the closet, Troy gathered the hangers, went back to the bed, and worked on hanging up the rest of his new clothes. When he finished, he stared at the closet, at his shirts and jeans sharing space with Jason's clothes.

Sharing space. He liked the way it made him feel. He'd never lived with anyone, not since college, and that had been just a roommate, not a lover. But he wasn't living with Jason, just visiting.

And Jason wasn't really a lover, was he?

Unsure, Troy frowned. Then he touched the leather thong at his throat, closed his eyes, and inhaled. The room carried Jason's scent, a soft male musk and citrus blend that, after such a short period of time, Troy recognized and his body reacted to.

It was crazy. This whole thing was insane. He'd lost his home, everything he owned, all the reminders and memories of a life he'd had before yesterday.

And for some even more insane reason he couldn't figure out, he looked forward to tomorrow. To what was coming, not what had been. And not to just when Jason returned.

To the rest of his life.

* * * * *

Jason bounded from his SUV and loped to his front door. Struggling to control himself from throwing the door to his apartment open, rushing in, and jumping into bed with Troy, he stopped on the welcome mat and took a deep, calming breath.

He didn't want to frighten Troy off. That was the last thing he wanted. The first thing was to lose himself in making love to the older man. God, his dick had been on alert since he'd ended his shift. With each mile closer to home, his growing desire for Troy had created a very painful yet sweet ache he knew would only be relieved by gazing down at the leather wrapped around Troy's tanned skin, at the skittering of

Troy's heartbeat while being bound, and at last, by sinking his throbbing cock deep inside Troy.

But falling on the man, tying him up, and ravishing him would not be cool, would it?

He let himself into his apartment and looked around. Part of him was frightened Troy would be gone. Part of him was frightened by the way Troy made him feel. Not the constant hard-ons. Or this new need to protect and possess. Despite the conflicting fears, Jason knew his body wanted Troy. Of that much, he was sure.

It was the fucking *happiness* that blew him away.

Like the way he'd stood by his car this morning and watched the sun rise over the flagpole outside the station, happy to be alive and living in Texas. How he'd sung at the top of his lungs all the sappy love songs on the radio during the drive home. Even right now, a pure adrenaline rush of happiness flooded his veins just knowing he'd see Troy again.

That was what scared him the most.

Because he knew when Troy's friends, along with Douglas, returned from their vacation, they'd take Troy away, back to his old life.

A life without Jason in it.

And that was it in a nutshell.

Jason without Troy. Fuck that hurt. That one thought.

And he shouldn't be having that thought. No way. They'd just met. Didn't really know each other. Sure they'd had sex. Usually, that meant nothing to him.

But the truth was, from the moment they'd met, Troy meant more to Jason than anyone had in like, forever.

He toed off his sneakers and took a bottle of water from the fridge as he thought his problem through.

Sure, he could tie Troy up, never let him go. But Jason didn't want a captive or want someone bound to him out of a sense of indebtedness.

If he wanted Troy to *want* to stay, he'd have to woo him. He'd never wooed anyone. Flirted, teased, even came right out and stated "let's fuck," but never chased anyone with such a serious intention as having a relationship.

Holy shit. A relationship?

Settle down? Hell no. But with a man like Troy, someone so responsive to Jason's desires, who was just exploring his own new responses, no way in hell would that be settling down.

It would be the biggest adventure of Jason's life.

He downed half the bottle in his first swig, then wiped his mouth with the back of his hand.

He didn't have enough money to really get Troy back on his feet financially, but from what the insurance guy had said, that wouldn't be a problem, it would just take time. And Troy had a good job, he'd told him that much during dinner at the restaurant. Besides, Jason couldn't really help him in that department, unless Troy wanted to train to become a firefighter.

Troy needed a place to live. Jason looked around. His place was small, probably too small for the both of them. He shouldn't be thinking of living with Troy. Would Troy even consider moving in with someone he'd met only a few days ago? He didn't think so, and he'd already resigned himself to helping Troy find an apartment, so he'd do it, despite his own feelings.

What Troy didn't have was the vacation he'd planned before the fire.

Jason's smile spread over his face as the ideas popped into his head almost too fast to register one before another took its place. If Troy had wanted a dream vacation, Jason would give him one.

The best vacation he'd ever had.

Chapter Twelve

After carefully closing the door to his bedroom, Jason undressed in the dark. He switched on the small lamp on his dresser and its soft glow gave off just enough light to see by so Jason didn't run into the furniture.

Troy slept, curled on his side, the pillow tucked under his cheek. The covers had shifted down to his waist, and from all the glorious skin and muscles Jason could see, he was naked.

Jason slipped under the covers and spooned Troy, pulling him close. He inhaled, Troy's scent flying through his system straight to his cock, and it filled.

Troy moaned softly and snuggled his ass into Jason's crotch. Jason's dick knew where it wanted to be; the damn thing roared painfully to life and claimed the narrow cleft of Troy's butt as its own.

Jason wrapped his arms around Troy, slipping one arm under his neck and the other around his chest. As he moved his hand over the silky skin and defined muscles of his lover's stomach, he buried his nose in his neck, licked a path to Troy's ear, then gave the soft earlobe a nip.

Troy groaned and pushed back into Jason.

"Been waiting for you. Don't tease me, Jas." Troy's need-filled voice made Jason's cock throb harder. This time, Troy wasn't dreaming about Douglas, he knew who his lover was, and that just about did it for Jason.

He rolled over, opened the drawer of his nightstand, and pulled out lube and condoms and put them on the bed next to him.

Troy made a needy little whimper when Jason moved, but as soon as he'd returned, Troy snuggled up against him again.

"Give me the lube." Troy held out his hand.

Jason gave it to him and Troy flipped open the cap, squeezed some onto his fingers, and prepped himself.

God, that was so hot, watching Troy ready himself to be fucked. It just made Jason's dick ache. He ripped open a condom and rolled it on.

"How do you want me?" Troy dropped the lube on the floor and looked over his shoulder at Jason.

"I want to kiss you and look into your eyes when I fuck you." Jason kissed Troy's shoulder.

Troy rolled onto his back and held his arms out for Jason. Jason fell into them as he kissed his lover. Their bodies rubbed together, cocks trapped between them, Jason's legs spreading Troy's apart. Troy's warm precum dribbled across Jason's belly.

He rolled to the side and, using his finger, delved into Troy's tight hole, earning a cry of pleasure from Troy. Jason worked the tight opening, letting his finger dance over Troy's sweet spot.

"Oh God, Jas!" Troy fucked Jason's finger, riding that spot with each thrust of his ass.

Jason shifted lower, his cock ready, and pushed Troy's legs up, tilting his pelvis into the perfect position for penetration. He removed his finger and positioned the head of his dick at Troy's opening.

Troy reached up and wrapped his arms around Jason's neck, his legs around

Jason's thighs, and pulled him closer. "Now. I want you now, Jas."

Jason plunged in, submerging his prick deep into Troy's tunnel as his lover cried out.

Jason gasped. "Oh shit, man. It's so good. So hot. Fuck."

Troy's ass burned, but he gulped down air and controlled the urge to push Jason out, letting his body adjust to the invasion. Jason wasn't as long as he was and only a little thicker, and although it stretched him, it wasn't painful.

Having Jason's cock in him was fantastic, so good it was unbelievable. He clung to Jason for a moment, then when the need rose to feel the slide of in and out, he nodded to Jason.

"Fuck, yes." Jason began thrusting, each slow push in, followed by a fast pull out, then a deeper push, fast out, until the pace had been set, and Troy matched it with his own body.

Troy lost himself in Jason's blue eyes, in the tremble of Jason's lip, the tentative bite of teeth to stop the tremble, the shuttering of Jason's eyelids as pleasure and arousal widened the dark pupils behind them.

If Troy had thought Jason a god before, then he was more than that now. Troy didn't know what more than a god was, but Jason was it. Youth, perfection of body, and a joyous spirit had been rolled into one incredible package in Jason.

What had he done to deserve Jason? To deserve life?

Jason moaned and, eyes closed, hung his head. Then his body tightened, and with a roar, all that coiled energy released, and Jason became a machine gun, delivering hot, rapid thrusts, destroying everything Troy had ever known about the act in a blind, hard, primal fuck.

All Troy could do was lie there and take the assault. His body pressed into the bed, his head thrown back as every staccato stroke hit his gland, pushing him toward orgasm. He couldn't even catch his breath to fight back and hold off coming, not for a second. His orgasm surged, hit the wall, and then overtook his body. He shot cum over his belly as he cried out, fingers digging into Jason's shoulders.

Jason shouted, "Troy!" and pushed deep and hard into his ass.

Then he collapsed onto Troy, burying his face in the crook of Troy's neck. Troy wrapped his arms around him.

"What the fuck, Jas? That was incredible."

Jason laughed. "Thanks." He rolled off and flopped back on the bed.

Troy got up, padded to the bath, and came back with a damp washcloth, then cleaned Jason and himself up. He tossed it on the floor and lay back down.

"Good morning."

Troy laughed. "A damn fine morning," Troy replied. He rolled onto his side and kissed Jason. They melted together, then parted.

Jason raised his arm. "Here it is, get a big sniff. We had a few calls last night, so I'm good and smelly."

Troy laughed, leaned in, and inhaled. "Damn. My favorite. Eau de Jason. Does it come in a roll-on?"

"Nope. Just the original." Jason slapped Troy on the ass. "Let's shower and get going."

"Get going? Where?" Troy sat up and ran his hand through his hair.

"After we stop at the bank to get your cards, we're going up to the lake. Put on some shorts and a T-shirt." Jason bounded out of bed.

Obviously, he didn't need much time to recover, but Troy wasn't as young as

Jason. He wasn't sure how much older he was, but right now, it felt like a lot.

"Hey, how old are you?" Troy asked.

"Twenty-nine," Jason called back as he disappeared into the bathroom. The shower started. "Come on. Daylight's burning."

"Twenty-nine, my ass. Twenty-five, maybe," Troy grumbled as he entered the small bath.

"Why? How old are you?" Jason got into the shower and began scrubbing.

"Thirty-four." Troy sighed and turned to his refection. Thank God he didn't have any gray hairs, his skin looked good, and his hair was still thick and full.

"That's only five years. Nothing to worry about, man." Jason rinsed off and stepped out. "Your turn."

The shower was barely big enough for one of them, there was no way they'd both fit in there for some shower sex. Maybe in Troy's new apartment, a bigger shower would be a priority.

"So, what are we going to do at the lake?" he asked as he took Jason's place. There were several lakes around Houston, Clear Lake in the south, and Lake Conroe and Lake Livingston up north. Jason had said "*up to the lake*," so it had to be Conroe or Livingston.

"It's a surprise." Jason began shaving at the single sink.

"I love surprises!" Troy hurried through his shower, rinsed, and grabbed a towel.

They got dressed and headed out the door.

"We'll pick up breakfast on the way up there. I know this great little place in Spring," Jason said as they climbed into his Explorer.

"Sounds good to me. I'm starving." Troy grinned.

Jason started the SUV, backed out, and took off. They made a quick stop at the bank. Troy's new credit card and debit card were ready and waiting for him, and it took only a few minutes to set his PIN and sign for them.

Before Troy knew it, they were on the I-45 heading north to Lake Conroe and whatever Jason had planned.

Chapter Thirteen

Around ten thirty they pulled up to the marina at Lake Conroe and parked.

Jason hopped out and headed for a small building near the docks and Troy followed. A large sign hung over the shack.

RENTALS
DAY OR HOUR
JET SKI   PARASAILING   CANOES
KAYAKS   PARTY BOATS

"What do you have planned?" Troy looked up at the sign. He and his friends had planned to snorkel on the cruise, but they'd never thought about renting watercraft. He looked out at the lake. Half a dozen Jet Skis bounced across the waves at what looked to him like ridiculously unsafe speeds.

"First, let's do the Jet Skis. Ever rode one?" Troy leaned on the counter and looked back over his shoulder.

"No."

"They're a fucking blast. You're going to love it," Jason assured him. "Hey, Dalton." He greeted the man behind the counter, and they shook hands.

"Jason! Long time no see. Where've you been, dude?"

"Working for the Houston Fire Department now. Not much time for fun these days." Jason shrugged.

"Who's your friend?" The guy checked Troy out. No sexual interest, just curiosity.

"A good friend of mine. He's never done this before. Thought I'd give him his first taste of the joy that is riding Jet Skis."

"Well, have fun. And don't be such a stranger, dude."

"Will do." Jason paid for the rentals.

"Let me pay you for it, man." Troy reached into his pocket for his new wallet.

"No way. It's on me." Jason waved him off.

"Okay. Hey, wait a minute. You said 'first'?"

"Ever parasailed?" Jason wiggled his eyebrows.

"No way." Troy shook his head. "I'm not sure about that."

"It's a blast. Trust me." Jason leaned toward Troy and lowered his voice. "I know you trust me, don't you?" He fingered the thong around Troy's neck and looked deep into Troy's eyes. The bones in his legs went soft, his dick went hard, and he had to fight to keep from taking Jason's mouth in a hungry kiss.

"Yes." Troy sighed and shrugged. "Whatever you say."

"Good." Jason turned back to his friend behind the counter, took the two wristbands, and handed one to Troy. "Put this on, and we'll go get the Jet

Skis." He helped Troy attach the bands and then they headed down the pier.

At the end, they showed their bands to a couple of young men who handed them two life vests. Jason helped Troy get his on, then slipped into his as if he'd done this many times before.

One of the guys led Troy to a bright red craft floating in the water next to the pier. It was bigger than he thought it would be, very roomy. In fact, the guy told him it held two people easily. It wouldn't be wise to suggest he ride behind Jason, but the idea didn't do much to lessen his arousal. After a brief explanation of the controls, the worker held the Jet Ski close to the dock with one foot as Troy stepped on and straddled the seat. It was like sitting on a large motorcycle with no wheels as it bobbed up and down on the water.

The man unhooked the rope, and Troy started the motor. The seat underneath him vibrated, and the engine quietly rumbled.

"Go slow until you're out on the lake, then just watch out for slower boats." The guy waved him off.

Troy twisted the handle, and the motor revved and moved him forward. He looked up to find Jason already way ahead of him. He increased his speed slowly until he'd moved far enough away from the dock for safety, then motored up to Jason.

"Ready?" Jason's eyes glittered.

"As I'll ever be," Troy shouted.

And with that, Jason took off with a loud "*yeehaw!*"

Troy laughed and let it rip. The Jet Ski surged, and he leaned forward as it skipped over the waves of the lake, wind blowing his hair as he followed Jason.

For an hour they chased each other around the lake. Troy imitated Jason, doing whatever the younger daredevil did. If Jason cut across the backwash of a ski boat, hopped the waves, went airborne, then slapped down on the water's surface,

Troy did it too. If Jason did tight circles, churning up water as he spun, Troy did it until he was so dizzy he couldn't focus.

What Troy did that Jason didn't do was take a spill. He'd cut a corner too sharp, and the Jet Ski turned on its side and he fell off. But he bobbed up just a few feet from the craft. With the automatic dead man's switch, the craft floated, idling in the water nearby. Jason pulled up beside him and held out his hand. Laughing, Troy took it and Jason pulled him onto his Jet Ski. Troy, soaking wet, straddled the seat behind Jason as they puttered over to Troy's empty craft. He took the opportunity to wrap his arms around Jason's waist and run his hands over Jason's well-defined abs. The younger man guided Troy's hand down to cover his crotch.

It didn't surprise Troy that Jason had the beginnings of a good-sized erection. It matched his. He moved closer and pushed against Jason's ass.

"Does riding a Jet Ski always make you hard?" Troy leaned closer and spoke into Jason's ear.

"Only with you sitting behind me, man. What's your excuse?" He pressed Troy's hand and rubbed it up and down over his hard-on, then let him go. "If you don't get off this ski right now, we're going to get in trouble."

"Thanks for the warning." Troy laughed, more than flattered he'd turned Jason on. He slid backward on the seat putting some space between them.

With just a little maneuvering, Troy managed to get on his Jet Ski and back into the fun. This time, he took the lead and led Jason around as they raced across the lake. Troy heard Jason's whoops over the sounds of the motors and the lake, and before he knew it, Troy had joined in, whooping and hollering and laughing like he'd never done before in his adult life.

If he'd known this was so much fun, he'd have done this years ago. It was wild, exciting, and just like Jason had promised, a total blast.

Jason headed toward the dock, and Troy followed. He didn't want it to end, but their time was up. They edged up to the pier, and the two guys hooked up the ropes to secure the craft to the dock. Troy climbed off.

"Man, that was a blast!" His clothes clung to him, and he shook the water from his hair.

"What did I tell you?" Jason grinned at him.

"I don't think I've ever had so much fun on the water." Troy walked beside Jason down the wooden pier to the rental shack. His sneakers squelched with each soggy footstep, but he didn't care about being wet. He'd dry out before long, and the temperature had climbed to the mid-eighties.

Jason made arrangements for the parasailing and returned with two bottles of cold water. He handed one to Troy. "Drink up."

It wasn't very hot, but Troy's throat was dry. They downed the water and tossed the bottles in the trash.

"Even though it's not summer, the sun on the water, the wind, and the heat really dry you out." Jason struck a weight-lifter pose. "And I'm all about hydration." Jason jerked his head for Troy to follow him. "The boat's over here."

They walked down another pier. There were a few other customers waiting in line to be taken up, so they sat on the dock, dangling their feet over the water until their turn.

"God, it's beautiful here. How'd you know about this place?" Troy asked as he looked around.

"My family's from Conroe. I grew up on the lake. In fact, when I was in high school, I used to work here during the summer."

Troy watched as the next person in line got on the boat. It motored to the middle of the lake. The woman rigged up and went over the side, her flotation device keeping her high in the water. Then the boat took off, the large chute behind her rose, lifted her out of the water and into the air. After a few trips around the lake, the boat slowed and the woman floated down, landing in the water with a soft splash.

"You're going to love this. The view from up there is awesome." Jason pointed to the boat.

"How high up do you go?" It looked pretty high to Troy. He'd already had his fill of heights this week, and he wasn't sure he'd enjoy this at all.

"Don't worry. No higher than that ledge you stood on." Jason bumped him with his shoulder.

"That's what I'm afraid of," Troy muttered.

Jason lowered his voice so only Troy could hear. "Hey, did I ever tell you how impressed I was when I first saw you that night? Man, you were fucking unbelievable, clinging to the side of the building with the fire shooting out of the windows around you. Shit, man, I got hard just looking at you."

"I was terrified." Troy shook his head. He could still feel the fear dancing in his belly.

"That's what was so great. What made it such an act of bravery."

"Bravery? Survival, more like." Troy snorted. He didn't think he'd been brave at all, just scared.

"Sure. You were frightened, but you did it anyway. Took the risk and got out on that ledge. I have to tell you, most people would have just jumped." Jason leaned against him and touched the knot on the cord around Troy's neck.

"Really?" Troy stared at Jason.

"Really. The flight urge takes over, and people jump. We see it all the time. Even though they're ten floors up, they'll jump rather than burn." Jason looked into Troy's eyes. "Fuck, I'm so glad you didn't jump."

Troy wanted nothing more than to lean in and kiss Jason, but this wasn't the time or place for a PDA by two gay men. Instead, he covered Jason's hand with his and gave it a squeeze.

"Me too." Troy winked.

Jason laughed. "Hey, we're up next."

Troy watched as the next person got into the boat, then into the water and then up into the air.

"I think I might puke." Troy groaned.

"Puke in the air, dude." Jason jabbed him in the ribs with his elbow. "Maybe you'll hit someone."

"Gross." Troy grimaced but laughed anyway.

The boat returned, and it was their turn.

"You go first." Jason pushed him.

"Hell no. You're going to get me up there and then not go." Troy pushed back.

"Dude. I've done this like a million times. Go on."

"Okay. But if I puke..." Troy went to the boat. Two guys ran the operation. One drove the boat, one spotted the sail. The driver was around forty, probably owned the boat, and his partner looked like his son, a teenager. Both of them had dark tans and wore sunglasses.

The kid helped Troy into his life vest and then the rigging for the parasail. Once fully outfitted, Troy got in the boat and sat on the side as it headed for the center of the lake. They got the sail and him in the water, moved away to take the slack out of the lines, then gave Troy the thumbs-up.

"God save me." Troy raised his hand and stuck his thumb up. The lines tightened, and before he knew it, the boat dragged him through the water a little ways, the water fell away and he was airborne.

"Holy shit!" he yelped. His feet dangled beneath him, and he looked down. He was higher than he'd been on the ledge, but this was completely different. This time he wasn't terrified; he was thrilled. Exhilarated. The view from his aerial perch above the lake was unlike anything he'd ever seen. It was beautiful. Dark blue water framed by a dark ring of pine trees stretched out all around him. Across the lake, he spotted Jason on the dock, waving at him.

He waved back, grinning like a fool.

The boat circled around and the sail carried him behind it. Wind blew his hair all over, whipped past his body, and he felt so light, as if he could stay suspended in air without the need for the boat and the parasail.

"*Yeehaw*!" he yelled as the boat swung near the dock.

"*Yeehaw*!" Jason answered in the distance.

Troy had never felt so connected to anyone as he did to Jason and it amazed him.

Everything he'd been feeling when he was around Jason astounded him. Everything felt right, as if this was what he was meant to do, and whom he was meant to be with. But it was foolish to think that way and dangerous to even think about letting Jason into his heart.

As the boat turned and he lost sight of Jason, Troy knew it would all be over soon. Jason was a nice guy. Gorgeous but nice, and when Troy found someone to take him off Jason's hands, he'd leave. And Jason would be happy to see him go.

Sure they were having fun, and Christ, the sex was phenomenal, but Troy was fooling himself to think this was anything more.

The boat came around, slowed, and his stomach dropped as he came down. His feet touched the water; then he sank under the surface and bobbed back up, the sail behind him. A few minutes later, he was back on the boat and heading to the dock.

"What'd you think?" Jason shouted as he bounced up and down on the pier.

"Fucking awesome!" Troy shouted, pumping his fist in the air. The boat pulled next to the dock, and Troy hopped out.

Jason met him in a bear hug and nearly spun him around.

"I told you! Just like I said, right?" Jason laughed.

Troy punched him on the arm. "Just like you said."

"My turn." Jason took the life vest from the guy and put it and then slipped into the harness like he knew what he was doing.

He got in the boat and turned to Troy. "Watch me!" he shouted just like some kid on the playground.

"I'm watching!" Troy shouted back and waved him off. The boat pulled away.

Troy sat on the edge of the dock and watched Jason take his turn around the lake.

They swapped waves, yells, and then, before he knew it, Jason was hopping off the boat and onto the dock.

Troy met him with his arms open. "That was so much fun. Thanks." He pulled Jason into a suitably butch man hug. They clapped each other on the back and then parted.

Together they walked down the dock toward the parking lot.

All Troy could think about was getting Jason alone.

Chapter Fourteen

"That was an awesome afternoon, Jas." Troy leaned back in the seat of the car and tapped his hand to the rhythm of the music on the radio.

"I loved your face, man. When you took that spill? I thought I'd pee myself I was laughing so hard." Jason pounded the steering wheel as he laughed.

"Hey. I could've drowned or been run over by an unmanned watercraft."

"No way. Flotation device. Dead man's switch." Jason shook his head.

Troy crossed his arms over his chest and looked offended. "Well…"

"And oh my God! You should have seen how big your smile was when the sail took you up. And sitting behind me on the Jet Ski? God, that was so hot." Jason made such a big show of adjusting his erection that Troy had to laugh.

"Does everything make you hard? Christ, you're like a teenager." Troy snorted.

"You love it, admit it."

"I'm not admitting anything that can be used against me."

"I'd like to use you against me." Jason growled and wiggled his eyebrows.

"Can you save it until we get home? If you keep this up, you're going to wreck the car." Troy pointed to the highway ahead as Jason slipped around a slower-moving car.

"Hey, you hungry? I could eat a horse." Jason changed the conversation faster than he changed lanes.

"Sure." Troy shrugged. "What did you have in mind?"

"I know this little place in the Montrose with the best hamburgers in town. It's just a grill, but the burgers are thick and juicy. They serve them wrapped in butcher paper to keep the juices from running down your arm."

"Sounds good. Big sloppy burgers."

"Then I'm going to need some sleep. Hope you don't mind?" Jason cast a sidelong look at Troy, and a twinge of guilt plucked at Troy.

"Look. I don't have to be entertained, Jas. Let's have dinner, and then you go to bed and get some rest. I'm just thankful I have a place to stay, really." Christ, he shuddered at the thought of telling Carlton what he'd done on his vacation if he'd wound up at some homeless shelter.

"Yeah. About that. I think we should pick up one of those little magazines for apartment rentals. They've got them at the grill. You can start looking for a new apartment tonight. If you see any, we can check them out tomorrow, after we go to the dealership and pick up the keys to your car."

"Good idea." Troy nodded. Well, Jason couldn't have made it clearer he wanted Troy to move along. He exhaled louder than he'd meant to.

"What?" Jason turned to him as they pulled up outside the grill.

"Nothing."

"Troy. Come on, man. Spill it." Jason turned the motor off and sat facing Troy.

"Really. Just tired. It was a long day." Troy rubbed his temple.

Jason leaned over, buried his hand in Troy's hair, and pulled him into a hard kiss. Troy's stomach dropped, and his balls tingled as Jason's tongue explored his mouth. Christ, he'd waited all day for this kiss, and it had been worth the wait.

"Gonna be a long night too." Jason sighed and leaned his forehead against Troy's as he fingered the leather thong around Troy's neck.

"Right. Work at the station." Troy nodded and got out of the car as Jason removed the keys and climbed out. They trotted over to the door of the restaurant and went inside.

"Sit anywhere." A young man with long, dark bangs called out to them. Troy had to do a double take, the guy was so gorgeous.

They slid into a booth. "Man, some scenery." Troy inclined his head slightly at the guy behind the counter.

"Yeah. Just forget it."

For a second, Troy's heart accelerated at the idea of Jason being jealous and possessive.

"He's taken." Jason tapped the ring finger of his left hand. Troy spotted the expensive-looking ring on the guy's finger. Someone had made sure his man had been tagged and off-limits to poaching.

Disappointment raced through Troy. Jason hadn't been jealous at all, just quick to check out the hot dude.

Jason tossed Troy a menu. "I'm getting a burger, fries, and a beer."

Troy checked out restaurant's offerings.

"What'll it be?" A gruff voice brought Troy's head up out of the menu.

Instead of the hot guy, an old man stood next to the table, order pad and pen ready. Jason sniggered and kicked Troy under the table. He looked back at the counter, but the hot guy had vanished.

Jason placed his order, giving Troy time to make a decision.

Troy closed the menu. "Same as him." There were just too many choices, and they all looked good.

The man scribbled on the pad, nodded, and headed back to the kitchen.

"Do you even know what I ordered?" Jason cocked his head at Troy.

"A burger, fries, and a beer?"

"Sort of. Burger, extra jalapeños, extra onions, bacon, and cheese."

"Damn, dude. That's a heart attack on a bun. You're going to have indigestion all night." Troy grimaced.

"So are you; you ordered it too." Jason tossed a paper napkin that he'd wadded up at Troy's face, and it hit him dead center.

"Hey!" Troy glared at his lover. "I may have ordered it, but that doesn't mean I'm going to eat it."

"What? Not man enough to handle a few peppers? Gonna let a little hot 'n' spicy do you in?" Jason dared as he leaned back on the bench and put his arms out, claiming his side of the booth. Christ, he looked good enough to eat.

Bring on the peppers. Troy licked his lips. "When you were a kid, did you just go around daring other boys to do shit for fun?"

"Yeah, pretty much. But I did a lot of stuff too. Had three brothers. We were pretty wild growing up. Conroe wasn't so built up, and we lived on five acres that backed up to the woods." He smiled at some memory, and Troy wished he could have seen that younger man in his glory. A fucking teenage Adonis, no doubt.

"Must have been fun. Are you the baby?"

The old man returned with their food, unloaded his tray, and placed the plates and beers in front of them. Then he gave them a nod and left.

"Nope. I'm in the middle. My kid brother just finished the police academy."

"Wow. A cop and a firefighter."

"Michael, the oldest, he's a Texas Ranger. The next one, Roger, is a marine serving in Iraq right now."

"You're all adrenaline junkies!"

"Sort of runs in the family." Jason laughed.

"Your poor parents." Troy shook his head as he squeezed ketchup from the bottle on his plate for the fries.

"You think? My old man is a retired Texas Ranger, and my mom, well, she's man enough to handle all of us, let me tell you." Jason's eyes shone with pride as he spoke about his family.

"Are you the only…?"

"One who's gay? No. Michael's gay too."

"Do your parents know?"

"Sure. Everyone's honest and open about it. The family is tight, man." Jason clasped his hands together. "How about you?" He picked up his burger and took a huge bite.

"Not much to tell. Dad's dead, Mom's in Phoenix, no siblings." Troy looked at his burger and considered removing the peppers and onions.

"Too bad about your dad." Jason bit his lip, furrowed his brow, and placed his hand over Troy's.

"It's okay. It happened about seven years ago. He had cancer." Troy gave Jason's hand a quick squeeze, then let it go. He didn't want to talk about it, not the year his father struggled through the god-awful chemo and radiation, not of having to bury his father and not about leaving his mom to take a position here in Houston when the company he worked for relocated.

"Look, if you don't want the peppers, take them off, but I'm going to have onion breath." Jason winked, bringing him out of his mood.

Troy picked up his burger, secured the paper tighter around it, and shrugged. If Jason could handle it, so could he. "Nope. I'm good." He bit into it, and juice dribbled down his chin.

As Troy snatched some paper napkins, Jason laughed. "Best burgers in town."

Troy looked across the table at the incredible man sitting in the booth with him and grinned. He could have been eating dog food as long as Jason was there with him, making him laugh and feel like he was a kid again.

He wiped his mouth and glanced around. By the door stood a metal stand holding several stacks of small books. One of them was for apartments. Maybe if he distracted Jason, he'd forget about it. At least for another day.

They finished chatting and eating. The young, hot guy brought their bill and put it on the table. "Pay at the register." His soft voice was sexy as hell.

Troy stared at the ring in the hottie's navel as it peeked from under a tight black T-shirt, then flicked his gaze to Jason. Jason's gaze met his, and they both sighed.

The guy wiggled his ring finger at them. "Sorry. Taken," he said as if he'd read their minds. Then he spun around and did a slow slink back to the counter, with Troy and Jason watching the way his ass moved in the tight, low-slung jeans he wore.

"Man. I got to eat here more often," Jason whispered.

"Me too." Troy nodded as he slid out of the booth and grabbed the check. "I got it. No arguments."

Jason held up his hands. "No argument."

Troy strode over to the register and paid the old man for their food. When Troy turned around, Jason had scooped up one of the little books.

"Hey, almost forgot the apartment book." He held it up for Troy to see.

"Right. Good thing you remembered." Troy groaned.

Okay, he got the message. Find a place and get out. Jason was just too nice a guy to come right out and say anything. He was right. Like they say, after three days, fish and guests should be thrown out.

But it hadn't been three days, had it?

Chapter Fifteen

Troy sank into the couch, the apartment book clasped in his hands. He should open it, get started on looking for that apartment. Jason probably wanted him to leave as soon as he either found an apartment or arranged for one of his friends to take him in.

Shit. He didn't want to leave. He liked it here. Liked hanging with Jason. Like sleeping in his bed, the smell of Jason and their sex perfuming the sheets. Troy's cock stiffened, and he gazed at the door to the bedroom.

Jason had gone in there to catch of few hours of sleep before his shift.

Troy missed him. And he was just in the other room.

Fuck, this wasn't good. He hadn't felt like this about Douglas. With Douglas, it had been pure lust. Hot lust, but just lust. God knew he'd wanted it to be more than sex. He wanted a man to call his own. Someone to share his life with, and he'd thought Douglas would be the one.

But if he'd felt the same connection with Douglas he felt now with Jason, there'd be no way he'd even look twice at Jason. And he had. More than twice. Long, slow, hungry looks. He'd even gone home with Jason, a total stranger.

Seriously. There was something wrong with him.

He put the back of his hand to his forehead.

Troy groaned as he recognized the symptoms. Rapid heartbeat whenever he caught a glimpse of Jason. Constant hard-on when Jason came near. Prone to laughter at the slightest joke Jason uttered. Inability to stop staring at Jason.

Oh. My. God. This was terrible.

He'd fallen in love with Jason.

Troy slid off the couch and onto the floor, the apartment book over his face, and lay there for long minutes as he tried to talk himself out of the truth.

No fucking way. He'd just met the man. Barely knew him. Hadn't even checked out Jason's MySpace or Facebook pages or seen if he'd posted an ad on the HotGayMen site. Or, like Carlton suggested, hired a PI to do a background check.

No, he'd been carried away by their phenomenal sex. Mind-blowing, take-me-up-against-the-wall-and-fuck-me sex. Tie-me-up-and-make-me-your-sex-slave sex. Completely caught up in the roller-coaster ride of adrenaline Jason had been feeding him on.

This was just some sort of survivor bond. Had to be.

He'd formed an attachment to the man who'd rescued him, that's all.

Imprinted on Jason, like some baby duckling.

After he left, it'd dissipate or evaporate or get sucked out of him when his mind returned to its right state. Whatever that state might be. Horniness. Lust. Need.

But it wasn't love.

Oh hell. No fucking way.

* * * * *

Jason rolled over and pulled the covers up to his neck.

He'd had to force himself to pick up that apartment guide at the restaurant. Every fiber in his body told him not to do it, to conveniently forget about it.

But he'd seen Troy's gaze slide over it too.

There was no way Troy would have forgotten about the book.

It was just as well. He was getting too attached to Troy, and that was not good. Not good at all.

But goddamn, Troy was so beautiful. That all-over tan, the plump ass Jason wanted to sink his teeth into and mark, telling everyone that Troy was his.

And the leather strap Troy let him tie around his throat? Just the sight of it made Jason's dick swell. And he'd just about come playing with it in the dressing room, and later in bed, with Troy looking up at him, surrendering to him, submitting to him.

He'd found the right man. A submissive willing to experiment. Maybe someone who'd let him get deeper into rope binding, Jason's secret fantasy. The ancient Japanese art of *Shibari* had been something he'd longed to try, ever since he'd seen photographs of it on the Internet.

Men bound in rope. Patterns that decorated their skin. Those black-and-white photographs had reached inside and spoken to him, rocking him to his core.

Jason's cock throbbed, begging him to touch it. The temperature in the darkened room had soared in only a few minutes. He pushed the covers off to give his body some cool air.

Oh God, Jason could just imagine Troy bound, arms behind his back, the beauty of the ropes making intricate patterns across his body. Wrapping around Troy's dick, climbing the valley of his ass, pulling tight.

Unable to resist, Jason grabbed his shaft and stroked. He shuddered at the image of Troy straining, struggling to get free, ropes binding everything but his stiff erection.

And Jason would swallow Troy to the root, until he felt the ropes that bound his lover against his lips.

Jason jerked faster, his balls tight to his body as the building orgasm pushed him to the edge.

He'd bend Troy over the sofa, and bound with his arms tied high between his shoulder blades, Jason would fuck him. Shift the rope up his cleft to the side and take Troy's ass.

Shaft in and out, the rope's slight burn against Jason's cock. Even with his eyes closed, it would remind Jason of its presence on his lover's body. Restraining him. Forcing him to submit.

He groaned as he came, warm cum splattering over his belly. He ran his fingertips through it as he slowly pumped with the other hand, bringing himself down from his heightened state of arousal.

"Troy," he whispered.

* * * * *

Troy looked up from the notes he'd been taking when the door to Jason's room opened. "Hi." He gave his lover an appreciative smile. Jason, his hair still damp from the shower, wore blue jeans and a dark blue T-shirt with HFD in white printed over his heart. Damn, he looked good enough to undress.

"Hey." Jason came over and stood at the table, looking over his shoulder, his hand resting on Troy's shoulder. "Find anything?"

"A few possibilities." Troy shrugged. "I thought I'd try a new area."

"Near here?" Jason bit his bottom lip, and his hand gripped Troy just a hair tighter.

"No. Closer to downtown."

Jason let him go, went into the kitchen, opened the fridge. He took out a juice and twisted off the cap. "Is that closer to your work?"

"Yeah. Figured I could save on gas and take the bus. It would make up for the higher rent."

"Maybe you could find a loft?" Jason suggested. "Go all trendy and upscale."

"No, thanks. Too rich for my blood." Troy shook his head. "I need a place just big enough..." He trailed off. Big enough for two? No. He couldn't entertain those thoughts.

"For what?" Jason leaned on the counter and locked gazes with Troy.

Troy exhaled. "For me. Just big enough for me. Don't like all that open space. How the hell are you supposed to decorate it?"

"Rugs. You use rugs to zection off ze areas, dahling." Jason's voice took on a Russian accent in a falsetto. "Bubbala, ve must go vit all fur. Un za cow horns. I can see it now. It vill be stunning!" He threw his arms wide open and his head back as he camped it up.

Troy laughed. "You're hired!"

"Of course I am, dahling. Of course I am." Jason minced his way across the living room. "Don't you just love vhat I've done to zis place." He spun, then landed with his hands on his hips and flipped invisible long hair from his shoulders.

Troy thought he'd fall off the chair laughing. "Stop. Please!"

Jason laughed, then flopped onto the couch and scratched his crotch, regaining that outdoorsy, surfer-guy attitude. "Dude," he drawled. "Don't wet yourself."

"Then stop making me laugh!"

"I like it when you laugh. I like the way your eyes crinkle and shine. Like you don't have a care in the world. Like—" Jason clamped his mouth shut.

Troy stood. He wanted to be next to Jason in the worst way.

He launched himself over the couch and landed practically on top of his lover. They both bounced as the couch groaned under Troy's body slam, almost throwing Jason out of his seat.

"Like what?" Troy leaned in, staring into Jason's eyes.

"Like you're happy," Jason whispered. He reached up and ran his fingertip over the knot of leather.

"I am happy." Troy grinned. "I'm alive. I'm not in a homeless shelter. I'm getting my life back together, thanks to you." He shrugged. "Trust me, I know it could be worse."

Jason frowned. "Right. That's a lot to be happy about." He leaned in and kissed Troy on the mouth, and Troy opened for him. Their tongues danced, then retreated; then they broke the sweet kiss.

"Right." Troy rested his head against Jason's forehead and bit back words he knew he shouldn't say. This arrangement was temporary, just a couple of guys having a good time, no strings attached.

The best time he'd ever had, and it'd only been three days.

"Time for work?" Troy asked as he checked the clock on the microwave.

"Yeah. Back in the morning." Jason pushed off the couch. "Don't wait up for me."

Troy tossed a pillow at him, but he snatched it and tossed it back. It sailed across the sofa and into Troy's arms.

"Be safe, man," Troy said as he clutched the pillow to his chest. Shit, there was that pain again, the one he got every time Jason left the room.

"I'm all about safety, dude." With that, Jason was out the door.

Troy got up and dragged himself back to the table and his notes on the apartments. He'd found five places that looked good. Three were closer to town and he could afford. One was near his old place.

And one, a large one-bedroom with a study, was only a few blocks away from Jason.

Chapter Sixteen

The next morning, Troy rolled over and reached for his lover, but the other side of the bed was empty. He sat up and stretched. The clock on the nightstand read ten after eight in the morning.

He slipped out of bed, grabbed a pair of briefs from the drawer, and padded to the bathroom to get dressed. He hurried, thinking perhaps Jason was in the living room, waiting for him to wake up.

Troy left the bedroom. "Jason?"

No answer.

He looked around the empty apartment. His notes were still sitting on the table where he'd left them last night. Nothing had been moved.

Jason hadn't come home yet.

Why did that fact lead to something that tore at his gut? And why did he not want to think about it or put the thought into words?

It was nothing. Jason was late, that's all.

Troy snatched up the TV remote, sat on the edge of the sofa, and turned the set on. Flicking through the channels, he found the local news and stopped. His knee bounced as he suffered through traffic reports, commercials, and the school lunch menu until he couldn't stand it any longer and jumped to the next channel.

Searching for anything that would explain Jason's absence.

Frustrated, he watched another run-through of the same news he'd seen before. Instead of calming him, it only made him more agitated.

There had to be a reason. A safe reason.

Not a deadly fire claims firefighter's life sort of reason.

No, not that.

Troy's throat constricted as if someone's hand clamped around it, and he couldn't seem to catch his breath. His body trembled as fear raced through him.

This was nuts.

Everything was fine. Jason was fine.

Fuck. Why hadn't he gotten a new cell phone? Why didn't he have Jason's cell phone number? Why hadn't Jason called?

The key scratched in the lock, and the door opened. Troy jumped up and spun around. "Jason?"

Jason closed the door behind him. "Hey, man. Didn't think you'd be up so soon."

"I just got up. Where've you been?" Troy sounded casual, holding back, not wanting to rush to the younger man, gather him in his arms, and hug him so tight it was he who couldn't breathe.

Jason sighed and toed off his sneakers. "Late night. We had two alarms, back to back, then just before the shift ended, we had to roll on a vehicle accident with medical."

"Wow. That sounds like a hard night."

"Not bad, really, but coming off the adrenaline high is a bitch." Jason waved it off.

"You need some sleep." Troy veered around the sofa and met Jason on the other side, near the bedroom door. "Don't stop here, go straight to bed. Do not pass Go. Do not collect two hundred dollars." He shepherded his lover into the bedroom.

"I'm not that bad." Jason laughed. "You're such a mother hen."

"I like to think of myself as an overprotective rooster." Troy gave him a peck on the cheek, then unbuttoned Jason's shirt and peeled it off him. Strong, sweaty man scent hit Troy like a hammer and shot straight to his dick.

That poor excuse for a kiss had done nothing for him, just made him want more, like his tongue down Jason's throat.

"Hey, we need to get your car keys and your car today. And maybe start looking at apartments," Jason argued, but he didn't stop Troy from helping to undress him. Jason unbuckled his belt, slid it out, then undid his jeans and pushed them down around his thighs. His cock bulged in his black briefs.

Troy pushed him down on the bed, pulled off his socks, then dragged off the jeans and briefs.

"Get under the covers." He picked up the rest of the clothes and took them to the laundry hamper in the bathroom and returned.

"God, you turn me on when you're being butch." Jason wiggled his eyebrows.

"I'm always butch, jerk," Troy shot back.

"Uh-huh. Wake me up later." Jason covered himself up and rolled onto his side.

Troy sat on the edge of the bed. "How much time do you need?" He brushed the dark bangs back from Jason's face, letting his fingertips dance lightly over his lover's skin.

Jason took Troy's hand, dragged it to his crotch, and groaned. "Fuck it. Sleep with me."

"Sleep?" Troy cocked an eyebrow as he slid his hand away.

"Well, maybe not." Jason chuckled sleepily. "Okay, wake me in three hours. That should give us plenty of time to get some stuff done."

"And by stuff, you mean get my car and look at apartments, right?"

"Sure, that too." Jason shrugged.

"Horndog." Troy got up and headed for the door.

"Troy?"

"Yeah?" He stopped and looked back.

Shadows hid Jason's face. "I'm sorry I didn't call. You didn't worry about me, did you?"

"Hell no." Troy laughed. "Mr. Big Brave Firefighter?"

"Okay. Didn't want to scare you, you know?" Jason's voice faded.

"You didn't," Jason lied. "See you in a while."

Troy smiled, then left and closed the door behind him. He leaned against the door and exhaled.

Damn, his legs still hadn't stopped shaking.

* * * * *

Damn, for a minute Jason thought Troy had worried about him, but guess not. Jason hadn't wanted to call about being late in case Troy was still sleeping, wanted to let him get some rest after all he'd been through.

But a part of him, the part he didn't want to admit, had wanted to know if Troy would miss him or worry about him or even yell at him for scaring him half to death.

He'd really just wanted to know if Troy cared.

Shit. Man, he was beat. They'd done some training when he came on shift; then he studied for an hour and had crawled into bed around one a.m. Then the damn alarm went off, and it had been *go go go* the rest of the shift.

Now, he could barely keep his eyes open.

He closed them and tried to let go, but something bothered him.

Disappointment.

He hadn't gotten what he wanted, and it tasted bitter in his mouth.

Troy hadn't been the least bit worried about him.

That sucked.

* * * * *

Troy kept one eye on the TV and one on the clock. It took forever for three hours to pass, and he'd finished looking through the rental book and had found enough to look at for now. Once he saw them, he'd decide to keep searching or take one. There was no rush. He still had three days left.

He called the dealership at ten a.m. and spoke to the service department about getting a new key and lock fob. When the parts guy told him it would cost nearly two hundred dollars, he thought the man was joking.

He wasn't. But Troy would need the VIN from the car. Then they could look up the records of the sale and make sure he got a key that would work on his car.

Jason would have to bring him back to his apartment.

Troy sat back and rubbed his stomach. He wasn't sure how he felt about going back to his building, seeing the ruins of what was once his home or the ledge where he'd clung to the building.

But he'd have to face it sometime.

Especially if he wanted his car back. And he did. Once he had his car, he could come and go as he pleased, not depend on Jason. As soon as Carlton returned, Troy would be able to leave.

The car equaled freedom and independence, as all cars do. But it also equaled loss. Well, that's how life worked. You had to give up something in order to gain something else, didn't you?

Of course he wanted to move on with his life, get it back into some sort of order. Next week, he'd have to return to work, ready or not, and having a car would restore a bit of normalcy.

Part of him wanted to stay dependent on Jason. A big part.

The part of him that made his jeans too tight, made his body ache every time Jason came near him.

Desire. Longing. Need.

Troy glanced at the clock. Time was up.

He rushed to the bedroom door, rapped on it, then entered.

Jason pushed up in the bed. "Hey. Morning."

Troy sat on the edge of the bed. "Hey."

"Come here." Jason reached up, wrapped his hands around Troy's head, and dragged him down for a searing openmouthed kiss.

Troy melted.

Jason rolled, taking Troy with him, until Jason lay on top. Naked and hard.

"Now it's a good morning." Jason humped against Troy, his hands clutching Troy's ass.

Troy moaned, and his eyelids fluttered. God, the man knew how to turn him on.

He pressed up into Jason, showing his own stiff need.

"It could get better," Troy rasped.

"I know just the way too." Jason nipped Troy's throat, then licked a line up to his ear. Taking Troy's earlobe between his teeth, he played with it, worrying it, driving Troy nuts.

His cock was leaking like a sieve, and all he wanted was to take Jason's ass.

"I want inside your ass." He stared up into Jason's eyes. He had no idea if Jason would bottom or not, but he prayed Jason enjoyed it as much as he loved topping.

"'Bout time, dude." Jason groaned. "Thought you'd never ask." With all the ease of a trained wrestler, he locked his leg around Troy's and his arm around Troy's back and flipped them over. Troy topped now.

Jason opened his legs, and Troy slid between them. "Let me get my clothes off." Troy couldn't get them off fast enough, and a few buttons on his shirt popped in his rush.

"Slow down, man. I'm not going anywhere." Jason chuckled.

"I know." Troy didn't want to give Jason a chance to change his mind. Finally naked, he lay down on top of Jason.

"This is nice. I like the way you feel on top." Jason looked up at him. He put his hands over his head and lowered his thick, dark lashes. Damn, he looked sexy and hot and wanton as hell.

"God, I want to fuck you." Troy's cock leaked a line along Jason's thigh. "I need the stuff."

Jason stretched, opened the drawer, got the lube and the condom, and passed them to Troy. "Prep me, babe."

Troy shivered at Jason's deep voice and the eagerness shining in his eyes.

He popped the lube's cap, squeezed some out, and then painted the valley between Jason's spread thighs. He danced his finger over the tight opening, playing over it, learning its wrinkled pucker, how if he touched it with the least bit of pressure, Jason moaned.

Fuck, Jason was so hot, almost begging him for it.

Troy slipped his finger in. For a moment, there was resistance; then it gave way, and he sank in up to his second knuckle. Jason cried out, grabbed his balls, and pulled them up.

"Oh shit."

Troy kissed Jason's chest, latched onto a small dark nipple, and flicked it with his tongue. Jason jerked beneath him. Troy pushed deeper and then eased out, back in, back out, setting a pace as he finger fucked his lover.

"More. Harder." Jason panted as he rode Troy's finger. "You know what I need, babe."

"This?" He crooked his finger and brushed over Jason's gland.

Jason shuddered. "Fuck! Again. Fuck, do it again."

Troy obliged him.

Jason humped Troy's finger until Troy thought he'd come just watching the beauty of the man as he pleasured him. Even the way Jason bit his bottom lip made Troy's dick stiffen to nearly unbearable hardness.

"God, you're gorgeous."

"Fuck me now."

Troy pulled out his finger, ripped open the condom wrapper, and rolled it on his engorged prick. He pressed it to Jason's opening and pushed.

Jason pushed out, and Troy slid past the tight ring, into the heat of Jason's tunnel. It clamped down on his dick, and Troy gritted his teeth with the pleasure.

"Move babe." Jason slapped Troy's ass. Even when Troy topped, Jason was in control. "Ride me hard."

Troy pushed up on his hands, pulled out, then slammed home. He battered Jason's ass, shafting in and out in hard, smooth moves, going deeper with each penetration as Jason moaned and writhed beneath him.

Short, fast strokes took their place as Troy's orgasm built.

"Touch yourself. I want to feel you come." Troy grunted. Jason's cock dripped precum on his belly. It was so fucking sexy. Troy wanted to lick it off.

Jason released the sheets he'd crushed in one hand and stroked himself. After a few quick jerks, he ran his precum-soaked finger over Troy's lips like it was lip gloss.

Troy licked it off and groaned.

"Like the way I taste?"

"Yeah. I do." Troy nipped at Jason's finger.

Jason returned to stroking his dick, only now he held it loosely and moved his hand with short, quick jerks. He exhaled, tossed his head back, and hissed.

"Close."

Troy angled his hips, leaned forward, and nailed Jason's gland.

"Fuck!" Jason crowed.

With a shudder, he erupted, spilling white ropes of cum across his belly; the muscles surrounding Troy's dick clinched and held him in unbearable tightness.

"Oh shit." Troy lost it and shot his load into the condom, his body spasming with each hard spurt.

Troy's arms shook, and he collapsed onto his lover.

Jason wrapped his arms around Troy and held him tight. Troy couldn't do anything more than remember how to breathe, and even that took him a moment.

"God, that was so good. Being inside you," he mumbled into Jason's neck.

"I don't usually bottom, you know." Jason ran his hand over Troy's ass in a light, tender caress.

"I didn't think so. I was afraid you'd—"

"I wanted you to fuck me. Been thinking about it all night long."

"Me too." Troy grinned at his lover, unable to hide his happiness about Jason's admission.

Jason slapped him hard on his rump. "Right. We need to get going."

Oh well, so much for cuddling.

"Sure." Troy rolled off and removed the rubber. He got off the bed and went to the bathroom to toss it away. Jason stumbled in right behind him and beat him to the toilet.

He emptied his bladder, then flushed. Troy took his turn, flushed, and they did a quick cleanup with a wet cloth, shaved, and brushed their teeth.

After dressing, they went into the living room and sat at the table.

"Where's your list? This it?" Jason grabbed the notebook from in front of Troy and spun it around so he could read it.

"Yeah. I found a few more. But first, I need to get my car. Then I need a new cell phone." Troy took it back, ripped the sheet out, folded it, and tucked it into the pocket of his jeans.

"Sure." Jason stood and moved to the apartment's door. "I can't wait to see the apartments."

Couldn't wait for Troy to find someplace else to live, most likely, Troy thought as he followed Jason out of the door.

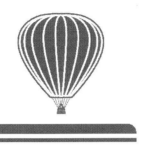

Chapter Seventeen

They pulled up to what was left of Troy's building. After three days, the place still stank from the fire. Yellow police tape blocked off the main entrance.

"Guess no one's allowed to go in yet." Jason shrugged.

Troy looked up at the third floor. Only a charred shell remained of most of the upper floors. The once-clean bricks were coated in soot and empty, and shattered windows dotted the front. There wasn't a light on anywhere. His gaze danced over to his apartment's location and landed on the small bathroom window and the ledge.

How the hell had he ever survived? And why him?

He shivered and rubbed his hands over his arms trying to warm himself. Jason threw his arm around Troy's shoulders and gave him a quick, hard hug.

"Sorry. This sucks."

Troy nodded, swallowed, and sighed. So much lost. He wondered if his neighbors were all right. He hadn't even thought about them until now. Maybe if he talked to the manager, he could find out. On second thought, he might not want to know.

"I hope everyone got out okay."

Jason inhaled hard. "Not everyone, man."

Troy looked at him. Oh shit. "What do you know?"

"Three dead from smoke inhalation. We got the report yesterday at the station."

Oh Christ. Troy started to shake. Jason held him tighter. "You're going to be fine."

"Three dead?" It was surreal. He couldn't reconcile it in his mind. People he'd known had died in the fire, and he'd been spared.

"The arson investigator said it started in the apartment next to yours. An old man lived there?"

"Yeah. Mr. Grunewald." Troy nodded. The retired factory worker had lived there longer than Troy. They would nod to each other in the halls, but Grunewald kept to himself.

"He must have been drinking. They found the bottle near his chair. He'd collapsed..."

"Jason!" Troy groaned. "Please. I don't want to hear it." Tears welled in his eyes.

"Shit, man. I'm so sorry. I didn't think." He bit his lip. "I'm just so used to talking about this stuff. It's my job, you know."

"I know." He didn't want to hear the details of the old man's death. Didn't want to replay it in his mind. He had enough nightmares of his own to dream about.

"Did you know him well?" Jason rubbed Troy's thigh.

"No. Not really. We said 'hi' and stuff. That was it."

Jason lowered his voice. "He didn't burn, Troy. He was dead before the fire reached him, if that helps."

"Yeah." Troy nodded. He didn't want to know about the other victims. "My car's in the parking lot around back." He pointed the way to the automatic gate that stood open.

Jason took his hand away, shifted into gear, and drove around the building to the rear where a dozen cars were parked.

"Which one?"

Troy pointed to a dark blue Altima. "That's mine."

"Nice car." Jason pulled into a spot next to it.

"I'll just take a minute." Troy got out, pen in hand, and pulled out his notepaper. The car wore a thin coat of soft gray ash. He avoided leaning against the car as he copied the VIN off the windshield. Then he hopped back into Troy's SUV and buckled up.

"The car looks good. No damage. Just needs a wash, that's all," Jason assured him.

"Yeah. After I get the key, I'll take it to the car wash."

"I'll take mine too." Jason nodded. "It needs a wash. And besides, if we go to one of the self-washing ones, I get to see you wet and soapy." He winked.

Troy rolled his eyes. "Horndog."

"You know me so well." Jason laughed.

They left and headed to the dealership.

* * * * *

After paying for his new key, Troy and Jason went back to the building and parked next to Troy's car. They got out, and Troy tried the key in the lock. Relief flooded him when it worked. He pressed the fob's buttons to check them, and the doors locked, unlocked, and the trunk popped open.

"Cool. It works." Jason grinned and gave him a thumbs-up. "Let's go get something to eat."

"Are eating and sex all you think about?" Troy asked as he opened the Altima's driver door to get in.

"Pretty much." Jason grinned at him. "Follow me." He ducked back into his car and pulled away.

Troy got in, cranked the engine, and it started right up. He followed Jason to a pizza place and parked. They went in, ordered a pizza, and devoured it. Maybe Jason had the right idea about food and sex.

"Now, I need a new cell phone," Troy said as he wiped the last of the pizza sauce from the corners of his mouth.

"What are you going to get?" Jason leaned back and looked him over. A wave of arousal rolled through Troy at the heated stare his lover shot him.

"Definitely a BlackBerry." Time to upgrade his phone.

"Dude. A BlackBerry? Can you spell boring?" Jason crumpled a paper napkin and tossed it at Troy, who batted it away. This time he'd been ready for Jason.

"What's wrong with it?"

"Get the iPhone." Jason held his out. "It's awesome."

Troy took it from him and studied it. He'd used it before but just to make a few calls.

"Look at all the apps. I can even get my e-mail."

"I can get e-mail on the BlackBerry. And it's not as expensive." Troy's practical side whispered in his ear, and true to form, he listened to it.

"Just look at what they've got when we get there, okay?"

"Sure." Troy slid out of the booth, and Jason followed. They paid at the counter and went to their cars. "Hey, let's not drive two cars all over. We'll take mine and park yours at your place."

"Good thinking." Jason nodded.

They drove back to Jason's, and he parked his car in front of his apartment and then got in with Troy.

"Still have your list of apartments?" Jason asked as he buckled up and adjusted the seat.

"Yeah." Troy tapped his pocket.

"Good. We should be able to see at least a couple of them before I have to get back."

Damn. Troy had hoped Jason would forget about the apartment, but no such luck.

"Right," Troy agreed. "Plenty of time left in the day."

They went to the phone store for Troy's carrier.

An hour later, Troy walked out with his new iPhone.

"I don't know how I let you talk me into this thing." Troy shook his head as he stared at the expensive toy in his hand. He'd spent way too much money on it.

"It sells itself, man. You're going to love it. Wait until you download your playlists."

"I don't have any playlists. They were on my computer and my iPod, both of which are nothing but a melted slag of plastic somewhere in my burned-out apartment," Troy grumbled.

"You can download some of my stuff. You can go through my library tonight while I'm at work, make your own playlist, and sync it up."

"All right." Troy snapped the phone into its new holder at his belt and pulled out the sheet of paper with the addresses of the apartments on them. "Let's do these first; they're near my old place."

"You're the boss." Jason trotted over to the car and bounced on his toes as he waited for Troy to get the doors open. Then he slid in, his hands beating out a wild drum solo on the dashboard.

Troy slid into the driver's seat and put the key in the ignition, but before he could turn it, Jason grabbed his neck with one hand and pulled him close.

"Kiss me," Jason demanded as he tugged on the leather strip around Troy's throat.

Troy obeyed, melting into his lover's embrace, melding his lips to Jason's.

Oh yeah. He was the boss. Not.

Chapter Eighteen

"**A**s you can see, it's quite spacious." The rental agent walked around the empty living room. "Two sets of built-in bookcases. And an eat-in counter for the kitchen."

Jason looked around. "You won't need a dining table." He shrugged.

"I prefer using a dining table." Troy didn't like this place at all. It wasn't right. Didn't feel good to him. Not like his last place. He'd known it had been right the minute he stepped foot inside.

"Let's take a look at the bedroom and bath, shall we?" She strode over to the door, leaving them alone.

"Shall we?" Jason bowed, flourishing his arm as if doffing his hat.

Troy shot him a glare. "She'll hear you," he whispered.

"Come on. I want to see the bathroom. I need to take a piss." Jason trotted after the woman.

Troy trudged along behind him.

God, he hated this. Finding a new apartment should be exciting, fun. Something to look forward to. So why did this suck?

In the bedroom, the woman stood with her arms folded, glaring at the bathroom door. From inside, Troy could hear Jason pissing into the toilet.

A loud "ahhh" of relief, followed by the toilet flushing, and a second later, Jason emerged as he zipped up. He grinned at Troy. "What?"

Troy just rolled his eyes and fought the urge to laugh. Jason was such a clown. He'd done that on purpose, just to rile the rental agent.

It had worked.

Her lips puckered and twisted. "Now, would *you* care to see the bathroom?"

Troy nodded and ducked into it. Single sink. Shower for one.

"Sorry. This isn't right for me."

She sighed loudly and turned on her heels to face him. "Maybe you'd like to see something else? A two-bedroom maybe?" Her gaze slid from him to Jason and back.

Jason walked over to Troy, slung his arm around Troy's shoulder, and pulled him close. "Two bedrooms? No way. We just need one." He smirked at her.

Troy smiled weakly at the lady.

"Well, this is the largest one-bedroom we have."

"Thanks for your time. I appreciate it." Troy swatted Jason across his taut abs.

She nodded and led them to the front door of the empty apartment. "Perhaps another time."

They thanked her and left. She followed them out, locking the door behind them.

When they reached the car, Troy turned to Jason. "Seriously. Could you have behaved worse?"

"What did I do?" Jason tried to look innocent, but he wasn't fooling Troy.

"Using the bathroom. We could hear you, you know."

"So, she never takes a piss?" Jason laughed, his eyes twinkling.

"It was a wonder you didn't try to have sex with me in front of her." Troy unlocked the doors, and they got in.

"I wanted to. But having a chick watch?" He shuddered. "That's just gross, dude."

Troy laughed until tears leaked. "Jas. You're killing me."

"Don't wet yourself." Jason pinched him on the thigh. "You'll ruin the leather."

When Troy got himself under control, they drove to the next place on the list.

* * * * *

"Three apartments, and none of them were any good." Troy slumped onto Jason's couch and leaned back.

"Too bad. We'll look again the day after tomorrow." Jason pulled a couple of beers from the fridge, opened them, and passed one to Troy.

"Why not tomorrow?" Troy took a sip. The cold beer chased the dryness in his throat away.

"I've got something special planned for tomorrow. After I get home, be ready." Jason wiggled his eyebrows and slugged back some beer.

"Ready for what?"

"Hot sex and fun, babe."

"Of course. Sex." Troy nodded. "I like the sex part." He really did. And with Jason, sex had been definitely hot. "What's the fun part?"

"Ever been deep-sea fishing?"

Troy sat up. "Deep-sea fishing? Are you serious?"

"As a heart attack."

"No. Isn't that expensive?"

"Yes. But I have a friend who owes me a favor. I'll call him tonight and set it up, if you're game." Jason pulled out his cell phone and waited.

Troy had been fishing, what kid hadn't, but deep sea? "Big fish, like marlin?"

"Sure. Marlin. Tarpon. Even sharks."

"Have you ever been?"

"Sure. It's a fucking rush. You're strapped into the chair and get one of those big motherfuckers on the end of a line fighting you all the way to the boat; then you bring it in. Man! That's un-fucking-believable." Jason's eyes lit up, and his entire body seemed to glow as he leaned forward as he spoke.

Just listening to Jason got Troy excited. And scared. "Isn't it dangerous?"

"Well, sure. That's the thrill. Knowing you could get yanked out of the chair or lose your tackle. You could even get hurt by the fish once it's on board. But that hardly ever really happens." He waved his beer.

"But it does happen?" Troy swallowed down a lump in his chest.

Jason just shrugged. "Should I call him?"

Troy looked at Jason. If he said no, what would Jason think of him? What would he think of himself? Hell, it was just fishing. He and his friends had planned to snorkel in the islands on the cruise. Was this any different or any less dangerous?

Hell, he'd clung to the side of a burning building. Parasailed and Jet Skied on the lake. And he'd had the time of his life.

"Sure. Call him. Sounds like a blast." Troy grinned.

"*Yeehaw*!" Jason hit some buttons on his phone and made the call as he paced around the apartment talking to his friend. Once the arrangements were made, he hung up.

"All set. We need to be at the pier in Kemah by nine a.m."

"What if you're late?"

"I'll call. Promise. Here, let's swap our numbers. I'll give you John's number for the boat, in case."

They sat on the couch and programmed in the numbers.

"I need to catch some sleep. Let's order in Chinese." Jason flipped through his numbers, hit Send, and placed the order. He glanced at Troy. "Twice-cooked pork okay?"

"And fried rice," Troy added.

"And fried rice. And an order of ginger-glazed wings. Right." Jason nodded and disconnected. "It'll be here in thirty minutes."

"Great. I'm starved. What's on TV?"

"TV?" Jason put his phone on the coffee table. "I have a better idea." He slid off the couch, pushing the table away, and knelt between Troy's legs. That was all it took for Troy's prick to fill.

When he reached for Troy's belt, Troy moaned. "This is a much better idea than watching TV." Jason nuzzled Troy's now-throbbing dick through the thick denim.

"Uh-huh." Jason had Troy's jeans undone. "Lift up."

Troy pushed off the couch, and Jason slid his jeans and briefs down to his knees. Troy's cock sprung free, standing straight up from his neatly clipped blond pubes.

Jason buried his face in Troy's crotch and inhaled. "Fuck you smell good."

"Do I?" Troy choked out as he watched his lover lick his balls, running his tongue over them, then suck one into his mouth. Oh Christ, he was going to come all over the place.

"Mm hmm." Jason nodded, pulling Troy's sac, then releasing it, only to snag the other one and make Troy gasp.

Troy weaved his fingers into Jason's hair as his hips surged forward. Jason let him go, then licked a line up the underneath of Troy's rigid shaft. When he reached the tip, Jason nipped at the stiff ridge of the crown and sucked the nerve bundle.

Troy cried out. "Suck me."

After wrapping his hand around the base of Troy's cock, Jason swallowed him down. Twisting his hand, his head bobbing up and down on the end of Troy's cock, Jason worked Troy until the urge to come built to exquisite heights.

"Gonna come, babe," Troy gasped.

Jason sucked even harder and faster, taking him right to the edge.

Troy's balls pulled up, his body tensed. "Jason! Oh God!" He exploded into Jason's mouth, shooting hot, creamy cum down his throat.

It was so good. Troy's mind blanked out, his body went limp, and he almost slid off the couch.

Jason laughed as he wiped his chin. "You're so hot, Troy. I love when you come. You just let go. Surrender. It's so sexy." He rose up on his knees and kissed Troy on the lips. Troy opened, and Jason pushed his tongue in, letting Troy taste his own bitter cum.

"You're delicious." Jason stared deep into Troy's eyes. There was something Jason had never seen before hiding in Troy's brown eyes. Something he wanted to see again and again.

And he hoped it wasn't just lust.

For a moment that seemed to go on forever, they just sat staring into each other's eyes, sinking into deeper depths. Jason wanted to say something important. Something that once said would change the relationship between them.

Something that would expose his deepest feelings and lay his heart and soul bare. And to him, it seemed as if Troy waited for him to say that something.

Jason opened his mouth to let the words out.

The doorbell rang.

"Chinese," Jason whispered.

"What?" Troy asked, blinking, the spell that held them broken. The moment passed.

"It's the delivery guy from the Chinese place." Jason stood. "I'll get it."

Troy nodded, pulled his jeans and briefs up, and arranged his clothes as Jason went to the door.

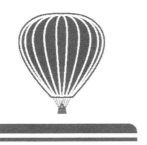

Chapter Nineteen

After they ate, Jason headed to the bedroom. Troy busied himself cleaning up in the tiny kitchen. He'd quickly learned where Jason kept everything, and there really wasn't room for more than one person working in it at a time.

The list of things he wanted in his new apartment grew. Definitely a larger kitchen.

He sat on the couch, picked up the remote, and scanned through the channels, and he settled on *The Deadliest Catch*. As he watched the men working in incredibly harsh conditions, almost being washed overboard, losing fingers, being beaten by equipment, he decided that probably hadn't been the best show to watch the night before their fishing trip.

Turning off the TV, he sat back and closed his eyes. The last few days ran through his head like a video. Man, he'd had a great time this week. Better maybe than the vacation he'd planned on, if that was possible.

All because of Jason.

The man had swept Troy off his feet, literally. From rescuing him to helping him rebuild his life, he'd been so giving, helpful, and funny, keeping Troy's spirits up. And the sex? Oh. My. God. The sex was the best he'd ever had. And he'd had more sex in the last few days than he'd had in ages.

More important, he liked the way he felt about himself when he was with Jason. As if there were no boundaries to his life, nothing holding him back, only his own preconceived notions about himself. This week he'd stretched those boundaries, explored his limits, and amazed himself at what he'd done.

Again, all because of Jason.

Troy touched the knot around his neck. Including this. To outward appearances, it was a plain black leather necklace, but to Troy it signified so much more. More than a piece of jewelry, a decoration, or some fashion, it was a constant reminder of his willing bond with Jason, the trust he held in the younger man and the commitment he'd agreed to for seven days.

Only a few days left before it came to an end, and he cut the leather thong from his neck, removing it and Jason from his life. Let him go and return to his normal life.

Normal didn't look so good anymore.

* * * * *

The alarm went off. Jason groaned and stretched. Man, his body was sore. Sure, he'd always enjoyed sports, the outdoors, and sex, but he hadn't done so much in ages. Especially the sex.

It was like he was sixteen again. A real horndog. Just like Troy called him.

Fuck. Getting older sucked. He'd be thirty in six months. Troy was five years older and had kept up with him every step of the way.

Jason sat up, ran his hands through his short-cropped hair, and looked down between his legs at the semihard shaft coming to life. His dick seemed to be stuck in perpetual "fuck" mode.

All because of Troy.

Man, it was like he craved the dude. He couldn't get enough of him, not the way he smelled, the way he tasted, the way he was such a goddamn perfect fit to Jason's body and cock.

But not for much longer.

Damn. He'd thought for a minute, before the delivery guy rang the doorbell, that something was going to happen to push their relationship to a new level. Something that would last more than just a few days of hot sex with no strings attached.

For the first time in his life, Jason wanted strings. And not just the ones he imagined he'd use to bind Troy, but strings that bound Troy's heart to him.

And that was stupid. That wasn't going to happen, and if he was smart, he'd put the idea out of his head before he got hurt. He'd never really had his heart broken before. Most of his relationships, if you could call them that, had never lasted very long and he'd been the one to break them off when the other guy got too close.

Looked like karma was going to catch up to him and kick him in the ass. With Troy, it would be Jason's turn to have his heart broken if he wasn't careful.

Jason made up his mind. He should cut his losses now, before it was too late. Tomorrow would be their last fun activity. After the fishing trip, it'd be back to business, finding Troy an apartment, and getting him packed up and out of his place.

And no more sex.

* * * * *

Troy looked up from thumbing through the apartment book as Jason came out of the bedroom. God, he loved the way Jason looked all clean and damp from the shower.

"Hey." He put down the book and moved over to make room for Jason. He'd waited hours to get his hands and lips on the man, and he was more than ready for a few kisses. Maybe he'd give Jason a quick blowjob to send him off to work with a smile on his handsome face.

"Hey." Jason detoured away and headed for the kitchen. He took a juice from the fridge and downed it. "Running late. I need to get going."

Troy frowned. It wasn't that late. "Okay. I'll see you in the morning."

"Right." Jason strode to the door and opened it. "Don't forget to download whatever you want from my iTunes library, dude."

"Sure. Thanks." Troy looked into Jason's eyes, searching for a sign to tell him what was up with his lover. Jason's gaze danced away from his.

"Night." Jason left. The door closed, and the lock snicked shut.

"Well, what the fuck was that?" Troy mumbled and fell back against the cushions of the sofa.

He rubbed his arms as a chill swept over him. Christ, he wanted to call Carlton and talk to him about everything that had happened, but Carlton's cell number was lost with his old phone.

Troy hurt. Deep down in his chest where air should be, he ached from the coldness of Jason's aloofness. Shit. He'd known this was going to happen if he got involved. He'd been kicked in the balls and left cringing on the ground.

He picked up the book and found his place.

Day after tomorrow, he'd pick a place. Anyplace, he didn't care anymore. The first place that said he could move in right away would do fine. He didn't plan on being an old smelly fish and get thrown out with the trash.

The fishing trip.

Troy groaned. It was too late to call it off, wasn't it? No, he could call the guy with the boat, John, and cancel. But Jason wanted to go and he'd been so excited about it. If Troy canceled, and Jason got pissed, that might be the end of any future chance Troy had with the firefighter, even though they'd never discussed what would happen between them once the week was over.

No strings attached. It'd be a clean break for the both of them. They'd had some fun, great, okay, fantastic sex, and good times. Jason had helped Troy through a rough patch. That's all.

Okay, he'd do the fishing trip. But that was it. They'd fish, come back to the apartment, and if there was still daylight, he'd go look at some apartments. Without Jason and his high jinks.

Sounded like a plan to him.

Troy got up, put the book on the coffee table, and sat at the computer on Jason's desk. He found the desktop icon for the iTunes library and opened it. Then he got his phone, the instruction booklet, and tried to figure it all out.

First he had to make a playlist. He followed the directions, named it *Troy's Music*, and started to go through Jason's music listings. There were at least a thousand pieces to choose from. Christ, just like the man himself, his music was all over the place. From jazz to gospel to thrash to—good God, Abba?

They definitely had different tastes in music.

After selecting a few dozen, he stopped. This wasn't right. Troy felt guilty about downloading music he hadn't paid for, so he closed it up and brought up the Internet. Going to the iTunes store, he created an account and searched through the selections, trying to replace the music he'd had on his old iPod.

After selecting nearly a hundred dollars worth of tunes, he did the download straight to his phone. Damn, that was cool. Maybe the phone wasn't so bad after all. It was still expensive, but the convenience was great, he'd give it that much.

He finished, put the phone on the charger, and decided to go to bed. There wasn't anything else to do in the apartment. Then he remembered he had his car now, and he could go out if he wanted. No reason he had to hang around here all night.

Troy changed his clothes, brushed his teeth, grabbed his phone, and without a look back, left the apartment. The door closed behind him, and he froze.

Oh shit. No key. He was locked out.

He'd never gotten a key from Jason because they'd always been together and he hadn't had a car before. He stood in the hall, unsure of what to do.

No problem. He had Jason's cell phone number. He could call and pick up the key later, after he'd gone out. Right now, he wanted to go out and maybe dance. Just like he'd planned with Douglas on the cruise. Dance the night away.

Jason trotted to his car, hit the remote, unlocked the car, and got in.

The night called. Music and dance awaited, and he was gay.

There had to be a party somewhere.

Chapter Twenty

"**M**y name is Troy."

The music in the club was too loud to talk over without yelling, so Troy gave up trying to hold a conversation. Besides, he wasn't here to talk. He looked up at the taller guy leaning against the bar and shrugged. He'd offered to buy Troy a drink, but he already had one.

"Let's dance." The man took Troy by the hand and led him to the dance floor.

Troy had had a rum and Coke, and he wasn't drunk by any means, just loose enough to break out some good moves. He moved with the beat of the song, a dance mix of upbeat Aretha Franklin tunes. Not too fast, not too slow.

The dude moved up behind him, put his hands on Troy's hips. Troy tensed at the possessive touch, then relaxed as they did a little dirty dancing. The crowd moved around them to the hard-driving bass beat, and Troy felt the guy's erection pressing into his ass. Oddly, it didn't do anything for him at all.

Okay, so he wasn't Douglas, he wasn't even Jason, but he'd do in a pinch. Troy wasn't looking for forever. He'd given up on finding that. It was a romantic fantasy. A gay man's myth. None of his friends had found forever, why should he?

The man's hands glided up his body, around his chest, and twisted Troy's nipples hard through his shirt.

"Ouch!" Troy brushed the guy's hands away. He turned his head, frowned, and mouthed, *That hurt.*

The guy lowered his mouth to Troy's ear. "Thought you liked it rough." Then he tapped the leather strap around Troy's throat.

Troy pulled away. "I don't know what you're talking about."

"Looks like someone's pet got off his chain." The knowing leer on his face irritated Troy.

Troy opened his mouth to argue, then realized he'd be wasting his breath and his time. He strode off the floor to the bar, leaving the guy alone in the middle of the crowd.

This had been a bad idea. He should have recognized that when he'd heard the door lock behind him.

He should go home. Well, back to Jason's place, anyway.

Troy spotted the guy coming toward him and decided now was the time to leave, so he ducked through the crowd, hit the door, and stepped out into the cool night air. He took a deep breath of clean, smoke-free air and headed to his car.

He slid behind the wheel and started it up. Maybe going out had been a mistake. He looked at the clock on the dash. Just after midnight. He pulled out his phone, scrolled down the very short list, and found Jason's number. After thinking for a second, he hit Send.

It rang.

Shit. What if Jason was sleeping?

Another ring.

What if he was at a fire?

Another ring.

"Hello?" Jason answered. He didn't sound asleep.

"It's Troy."

"Troy? What's up, man?" Now he sounded worried.

"I locked myself out of the apartment." Troy didn't want to explain what he'd done. Actually, he didn't want to explain why he'd done it. That would really sound lame. *Hey, man. I was so hurt by your brush-off, I went out to a bar and tried to get picked up.* Yeah, that sounded lame.

Jason chuckled. "How'd you do that, man?"

"I went out. I forgot I didn't have a key."

"Oh." Jason paused.

Troy winced, hoping Jason wouldn't pursue it further.

"Well, I'm at the station. You can come by and pick up the key."

"You sure?"

"Of course I'm sure. What? I'm going to make you sit in your car all night? Come get the key, dude." Now he sounded pissed.

"Okay."

"Where are you?"

"On Westheimer." Troy should have just said *at a gay bar* instead.

"Right." Jason gave him the directions to the station and hung up.

Troy put the car in gear and pulled away from the bar.

Twenty minutes later, Troy drove the back of the fire station, parked next to the other cars, and got out.

Jason stood against the back of the building, waiting for him. Another man was with him, standing a little too close for Troy's comfort. Okay, so he was jealous.

"Hey." Troy waved as he walked up to them.

Jason waved back. "Hey. Here's the key." He held it out but didn't move any closer.

Troy stepped up and took the key. "Thanks."

"Who's your friend, Cooper?" The stranger moved forward, checking Troy out. He was older, maybe fifty, with a shaved head that made him look like a bullet, and he was built like one too.

Jason hesitated; his gaze darted to Troy's face. Okay. So the men here at the station didn't know Jason was gay.

"I'm a friend of a friend. I'm having my house tented for termites, so Jason was nice enough to let me crash on his couch." Troy shrugged, not offering his hand or his name.

Jason smiled, looking relieved.

"Really?" The guy shot Jason a look that Troy couldn't read. Maybe he didn't believe Troy's answer, and that pissed Troy off. Even if it was a lie.

"Why does that surprise you?" Troy asked, getting a little defensive. "Jason's a firefighter. It's his job to rescue people."

Jason laughed. "Right, dude. I'm everyone's hero." He made muscles in his arms like some prizefighter, and Troy laughed.

"So you got locked out?" the man asked. Who did this guy think he was, the Grand Inquisitor?

"Yeah." Troy nodded and shoved the key in the pocket of his jeans. He wanted to shove the key down the guy's throat, but then he wouldn't have the key and he'd get his ass kicked. The old man looked tough as nails.

"Hitting the bars?" Maybe he did know Jason was gay. Maybe not, but Troy wasn't going to out Jason or anyone else.

He shrugged and took on a little of Jason's persona. "No... Made a beer run, dude. Got a couple of six-packs of Corona. Figured it was time to restock the fridge since I'd drunk up most of my host's inventory."

"Thanks, man." Jason looked relieved at the way Troy handled it.

"Dude." Troy rolled his eyes. "Thanks for the key."

Jason nodded. "No problem. I'll just ring the bell when I get home, okay?"

"Sure. I'll be up by then." Troy looked into Jason's eyes and saw a flicker of what he'd seen before last night, and it went straight to his dick.

"Great." Jason waved and headed back inside.

The guy stood there for a second, checking Troy out, then followed.

What the hell was up with that? Man, Jason would have to explain who that guy was.

As Troy got into the car, he remembered he'd have some answering to do himself in the morning. And he wasn't looking forward to that.

* * * * *

"A friend of a friend, huh?" Lieutenant Morris looked at Jason, expecting an answer.

Jason grinned and bounced the toe of his boot on the floor. "Well, not exactly."

"So, that's who's been putting that goofy grin on your face this week?" Morris shook his head.

"Yeah. That's him." Jason was thankful Morris was cool about him being gay, but then, Morris's youngest son was gay. It was a smaller world than most people thought.

"He seems nice. He lied for you." Morris chuckled.

"Yeah, he did."

"So? He's moved in?"

"Not exactly." Jason didn't want to explain about Troy or starting a relationship, or whatever they were having, with someone he'd rescued. That might be over the line.

"But he's staying at your place?"

"Yeah. Just for a few more days. Then he's getting his own place." Jason strode over to the truck, grabbed the rag he'd left on the table when Troy had called, and went back to shining the chrome.

Morris followed. "Where'd you meet?"

Damn. He wasn't going to let this go. Jason exhaled and turned around to face his boss. "I rescued him. On the ladder. The apartment fire last weekend? He didn't have anywhere to go, no friends in town, so I offered my place. Okay?"

Morris regarded him for a moment as Jason held his breath.

"That was a good thing to do, son." He clapped Jason on the shoulder. "I hope it works out for you."

Jason grimaced, tossed the rag to the floor, and threw up his arms. "Well, it's not going to. He's going to take an apartment and move out, get on with his life." He stared at the rag, sighed, then bent over and picked it up. Jason ran it through his hands, then went back to polishing.

"Does he know how you feel about him?"

"No." Jason shook his head. "It just got out of hand, man. Totally. And I really screwed it up last night, even if he wanted to stay."

Morris laughed. "Jeez. Just tell him you like him. He looks like he likes you."

Jason opened his mouth to say *the sex is hot* but thought that was not a conversation he wanted to have with his boss, even if the guy was like a second father to him. He wouldn't want to have it with his dad either. His brother Michael would understand, but he was up in Dallas. Maybe he'd call him tomorrow and see what he said.

"No. I think he needs to decide what he wants to do without any influence from me." Jason couldn't get past the notion that Troy was just going along with it to pay him back. And that wasn't what he wanted to base his first serious relationship on.

"Okay. Do it your way. But you know it's all right to admit you have feelings for someone." He chuckled. "I thought you gay guys were in touch with your emotions."

"That's a stereotype, Lieutenant. We're still guys." Jason shrugged.

"Well, get back to work. That engine isn't going to shine itself." Morris walked off.

"Yes, sir." Jason snapped the rag against the engine.

Chapter Twenty-one

Troy paced the living room waiting. He never called the boat guy to cancel, and he'd showered and dressed for the fishing trip. Now, all he needed was Jason to come home. No, that didn't sound right, but it did, and he knew it shouldn't.

The bell rang, and Troy threw himself at the door. At the last second, he stopped, took a deep breath, held it, and then let it out. He opened the door.

Jason stood there, bouncing his toe on the ground.

"Hey." He looked into Troy's eyes, and Troy melted. He reached out, grabbed Jason by the shirt, and pulled him inside, kicking the door closed.

Then he took Jason's mouth in the most passionate kiss of his life, throwing everything he had into it. Jason grabbed his ass and pulled him even tighter, rubbing his hardness against Troy's erection, giving as good as he got.

God, they rutted like animals in the hallway, and Troy loved it.

They couldn't keep denying there was something between them, could they? He wanted to spill it, tell Jason how he felt about him, but he still wasn't sure. So he held back, afraid to get hurt.

But Christ, the way Jason held him, kissed him. No one had ever made him feel the way Jason did, and he didn't want it to end.

Jason flicked his tongue over the roof of Troy's mouth, moaning and grinding their dicks together. Troy pushed him against the wall, shifted his grip on Jason to his head, and repositioned his mouth against Jason's lips.

"I missed you," Troy whispered. He felt famished without Jason's touch.

"Missed you too." Jason licked up Troy's neck; then his teeth took the leather and tugged on it.

Troy laughed and leaned back, enjoying the way the pull of the leather felt against his skin. They reluctantly broke apart.

"We need to get going," Troy reminded his lover.

"Okay, dude. Don't rush me." Jason pushed off the wall and headed to the bedroom. "Just give me twenty minutes."

"That long? What are you going to do in there, and can I help?" Troy wiggled his eyebrows at Jason as he followed him into the bedroom and plopped down on the bed.

"If I let you, we'd never make the boat in time. John'll be pissed if we get a late start." He ducked into the bathroom and shut the door.

Troy sighed. Everything seemed back to the way it had been. With any luck, he wouldn't have to explain last night. He waited, listening to the shower run, the toilet flush; then the door flew open and Jason strode out, naked and glorious and semihard.

"Damn." Troy groaned and rubbed his own cock through the cargo shorts he wore. It'd been ready for action since they'd kissed.

"Hold that thought until we get back." Jason pulled a pair of briefs out of his drawer and then pulled them on, adjusting himself. Troy watched, practically drooling, as his lover dressed in khaki shorts, a loose Hawaiian shirt, and boat shoes.

"We look like twins," Troy said, his hand sweeping over the khakis, light blue T-shirt, and sneakers he wore. He tossed a pillow at Jason, scoring a direct hit in the stomach.

"Well, I'm not changing. We'll just have to go to the dance in matching outfits." Jason tossed imaginary hair over his shoulder. "Let's go. The fish are waiting."

Laughing, Troy rolled to his feet and followed Jason out of the apartment.

* * * * *

They'd stopped at a fast-food place and ordered breakfast to go, then got back on the road. After about twenty minutes of quiet munching and chewing their sandwiches and slurping coffee, Jason couldn't stand it anymore. He cleared his throat. It was time he asked some questions and got some answers, no matter how bad they might hurt.

Ever since he'd spoken to Troy on the phone about the key, he'd known Troy had gone out to a gay bar. And after the way he'd treated Troy, freezing him out, Jason couldn't really blame him. But damn, it still hurt.

And what hurt even more was not knowing whom Troy had found at the club and what he'd done with him. Not knowing had been driving him crazy, although knowing might not be much better.

"So, where'd you really go last night?" He bit his lip and glanced over at Troy.

"To a club on Westheimer." Troy shrugged.

"Look, it's none of my business, and I know that, so just tell me to get fucked, but did you meet anyone there?"

"I danced with this guy. That's all," Troy said.

"Like I said, it's none of my—"

"I danced with him; then he got a little rough, so I left." Troy fingered the leather strap. "Seems wearing this thing is like chumming the water to a Dom." Then he gave a little laugh.

"Oh fuck! I should have warned you. Wearing that and going out without me to get between you and other Doms isn't a good idea."

"Hey, I can take care of myself. I managed fine." Troy huffed and crossed his arms. "And what the hell is this thing, anyway? A Dom homing beacon?"

"They thought you were advertising."

"Duh. I was at a gay bar. I was dancing. What part of that *isn't* advertising?" Troy exclaimed.

"I know. But it brings in some really, let's say, more dominant types. Men who don't mind getting a little rough if they think you're into it. I'm sorry."

"He said I'd slipped my chain." Troy chuckled. "Really, if I think about it, it's sort of funny."

"I don't think it's funny." Jason frowned. His sub had been hit on, and it pushed every Dom button in his body. "If I ever find that guy, I'm gonna kick his ass for touching you."

A hard tremor of lust shot through Troy's body at Jason's declaration of possession. He shouldn't like it, but he did.

"Really? You'd kick someone's ass for me? That's so sweet."

Jason laughed. "Yeah. But only for you, dude. As long as you wear that, you belong to me, and it's my responsibility to keep you safe, no matter what. Even if you get pissed at me and go out to a club looking for some action." There he'd said it, laid his fear right out there for Troy to see.

"About that." Troy cleared his throat. "You're right. I was pissed. And hurt."

"Sorry." Jason touched Troy's thigh. "I was wrong to treat you like that. I don't know what got into me."

Troy looked out the window for a long time. "It's okay. Look, in two days I'll be out of your life. Let's just have a good time until then. No strings."

Jason bit his lip. Well, it's what he'd agreed to in the beginning. It didn't matter that it had changed for him and not for Troy.

"Right. No strings." Time to change the subject. "Bet I catch a fish before you do, and I bet mine's bigger."

"You're on. What's the bet?"

"Loser has to bottom." Jason winked at Troy.

"I'm not sure I'd consider that losing." Troy shook his head.

"Me either." He shrugged. "But we could pretend."

Troy laughed.

* * * * *

They pulled up to the marina at Kemah and parked. Jason seemed to know where they were going, so Troy just followed along. All around them, boats of all sizes and types were moored against the piers jutting out into the small waterway that led to the bay, then out to the Gulf of Mexico.

"There's John," Jason said over his shoulder. He waved to a man standing on the dock, and the guy waved back. Tan, athletic, and good-looking, he looked to be in his forties.

They met, and John pulled Jason into an embrace. "Hey, Jas. It's been too long."

Jas? Troy's jealousy reared up and took a bite out of his ass.

"John, this is Troy Hastings, a good friend of mine." Jason grinned at him, and Troy smiled at John. It was clear the two men had real affection for each other, but it didn't look to be sexual, so Troy relaxed.

"Any friend of Jas's is a friend of mine." John nodded and shook his hand. His grip was firm, his hands callused but still gentle. Despite being jealous, Troy liked John.

"Jason says we're going to catch some big fish today." Troy punched Jason on the arm.

"He's right. The tarpon are running good right now, so are the marlin, but they're farther out than we're going to go." John turned and led the way down the pier.

Jason practically bounced down the wooden boards as he followed. "Think we'll hook any shark?"

"Might. We usually catch at least one or two." John shrugged.

The music from *Jaws* played in Troy's mind, and his stomach rolled. "Is the boat big?"

John stopped and turned around. He laughed loud and hard. "Yeah, it's big enough." He sobered and pinned Troy with his stare. "Do you get seasick? I don't want anyone barfing all over the deck."

Troy grimaced and rubbed his belly. "Can you get seasick on the dock?"

Jason giggled. "Sorry, John. He's a deep-sea fishing virgin."

"That's okay. I've got some Dramamine on board. He can take some right now before we get underway."

"Good." Troy nodded. He'd already started to feel queasy, and they hadn't even left the dock. He didn't want to spend the trip hanging over the side of the boat. Now that would be embarrassing. Jason would never let him live it down.

Then he remembered in two days, he'd be out of Jason's life.

They reached the end of the pier and stopped. Troy looked up at a huge boat. A metal ladder to climb up to the rear deck hung over the side. There was a deck on the front, and a tower that he figured John used to drive the boat. Do you drive boats? No, it was called steering, wasn't it? And which side was port and which starboard?

The name across the rear of the boat read *Gulf Star*. It really was a pretty boat. He should be absolutely safe, right? Would he look like a pussy if he asked about the life jackets?

John went up the ladder and swung his leg over the side, then disappeared.

Jason stood next to the ladder and motioned for him to go next. "Come on, dude. Let's get aboard."

Troy put his foot on the first rung and then looked back at Jason.

"Odd. You. Me. A ladder. This seems strangely familiar."

Jason burst out laughing and slapped him on the ass. "Get up there."

Troy obeyed his Dom and climbed up.

Chapter Twenty-two

"**D**o I look like a total pussy wearing this life vest?" Troy asked Jason.

"No." Jason snickered, and Troy shot him a glare. "Yeah. But that's okay." Jason leaned against the side of the boat as they cut through the bay to open water. He looked gorgeous against the light blue sky and dark water. It was a glorious morning, a little cool, but it'd be warming up soon. Gulls swooped and cawed overhead, and the smell of ocean filled the air.

Thank God the water was pretty calm, and after he'd taken the Dramamine pills, his stomach had settled down. John was up on the bridge, Jason had informed him of the technical term, and they were at the back of the boat where two large chairs were bolted to the deck. Jason explained what was going to happen once they hooked a fish.

"So, you'll get strapped in. You should like that." He grinned at Troy and then dodged his fist as he tried to land a punch. Jason stuck out his tongue.

"God, Jas. You're such a dude." Troy laughed.

"That's me. Butch all the way." Jason walked over to the stern. "See these poles? Those are the fishing rods." Troy looked up at them. They certainly looked like they could land a big fish. "John will bait them and then toss them over."

"Is he going to chum the water?"

"Maybe, maybe not. Depends on how deep the fish are running."

Jason looked out over the water; then his arm flew up as he pointed. "Dolphins!"

Troy rushed to Jason's side. About two hundred feet off the rear of the craft, several dolphins crested, dived, and crested, their backs and dorsal fins breaking the water, just like he'd seen in all the nature shows.

"Beautiful!" Troy leaned against Jason, and his lover wrapped an arm around his shoulder.

"What about John?" Troy whispered. He didn't know how much John knew about Jason.

"He's cool. He knows I'm gay."

"What about me?"

"I think he knows you're gay too." Jason reached down and goosed Troy, then leaned over and bit Troy's ear.

Troy squeaked and rubbed his ass. "Is John gay?"

"On occasion." Jason shrugged.

"Were any of those occasions with you?" Troy stared into Jason's eyes.

"No. He's a friend of a friend. We've all hung out together lots, though. Don's a good guy too, just like John," Jason assured him.

"Don and John?"

"Yeah. But they have this thing, you know?"

"A thing?" Troy shot a look over his shoulder at John standing in the bridge steering the boat.

"They don't live together during the week, but on the weekends, they live here on the boat. Don's got a loft downtown. He's a lawyer and makes big money. John used to be a lawyer, but he retired and runs the boat full time."

"Wow. How do you know all these people?"

"I met Don through my older brother Michael. He was working a case with Don. We all just hung out."

Troy smiled at Jason, and Jason leaned over for a quick kiss, but Troy had a different idea. He wrapped his hand around Jason's head and pulled him closer for more. Jason had just opened up to him when the sound of a throat clearing broke them apart.

"Hey, guys. Time to throw out the lines." John stood behind them, his arms crossed and a huge grin on his tanned face. "Come on, Jas. You can help me bait the hooks. I've got the poles geared up."

Troy sat in the chair. "Do you need me to help too?"

"No, it's cool." Jason and John carried a large cooler that had been sitting off to the side at the back of the boat and opened it. Inside, were several rows of fish on a bed of ice. John pulled a machete out and began cutting the fish in half on a wooden chopping block. Then Jason took the pieces and baited the huge hooks with them.

"Those are really big hooks," Troy remarked. They looked dangerously wicked sharp. If one of those caught you, you'd definitely need a doctor to remove it.

"Have to be to pull in these monsters," John replied.

Monsters? Troy gulped. Jason looked up and caught his eye.

"Don't worry. It's going to be a blast." He gave Troy a sexy grin.

Okay, it was official. Jason was a god. How anyone could manage to look sexy while baiting a hook with dead fish pieces, Troy would never know, but Jason managed to do it.

After the hooks were baited, Jason and John tossed them overboard, letting the lines run out, then stopped them. They placed the rods in holders on the back of the boat.

"Now we wait. When we get a hit, the action starts." John brought a bucket and bar of soap out and placed them on the deck. He scrubbed the soap over his hands and up his arms, then passed it to Jason, who did the same. Then John dumped the clean water over their arms, rinsing off the soap and fish smell.

Jason sat in one chair, Troy in the other, and John disappeared below deck.

"How long does it take?" Troy watched the place where the lines entered the water.

"Sometimes hours. Sometimes minutes. Just depends."

John returned with a metal bucket filled with ice and Coronas and passed one out to each of the guys. Troy twisted off the cap of his and took a sip.

"Man, that's good." Jason smacked his lips. "Cold beer and fishing. They just go together."

"Sure do." John leaned forward and held up his bottle in a toast. "To a good trip, good catch, big fish, and safe waters."

The guys all bumped bottles and took a drink.

The first pole's reel sang as something took the hook and ran with it.

"Let's go!" John yelled, stuck his beer back in the ice, and launched himself at the pole. He pulled it out of the holder and began cranking the reel. "Who's taking the first one?"

"Jason!"

"Troy!"

They sang out as they crammed their beers into the ice.

"Someone get strapped in!" John ordered.

Jason turned to Troy. "You go first. In case we don't get another hit, man." He pushed Troy back into the chair and began to strap him in. Troy's heart raced, thudding hard in his chest, as the sounds of the line playing out and being cranked back in filled the salty air and Jason rushed to snap the buckles on the harness that held him in the chair.

"He's in!" Jason shouted as he finished.

John walked backward, teeth clenched, the rod braced against his thigh as he fought the fish. He got the heel of the rod in the holder on the floor between Troy's legs and then hooked the rod to the straps of the chair.

Troy grabbed the rod and the shock of the fish fighting on the other end sent waves shuddering through his arms. "Oh my God!"

The fish pulled, and Troy bent forward as the rod bowed. Jason came up behind him and took the rod in his hands.

"Lean back!" He helped Troy pull back on the rod. "When you go forward, crank it! Get your feet in the stirrups!" Troy put his feet in the metal holders and braced himself against them.

They'd gone as far back as they could; then the fish pulled again, and they fell forward.

"Crank it!" Jason yelled in his ear.

Troy cranked the reel, the spinner going around and around until it wouldn't budge. Again, they pulled back. It was like he had blinders on. The world shrank to just the area straight ahead of him. Water, rod, line, and horizon.

Troy got into the rhythm of the fish as it went deep, came up, fighting the hook and line. Pulling back, going forward, winding in the line, then repeating it over and over until he thought his arms would fall off.

"This fish better be worth it," Troy muttered between his clamped jaws. Sweat poured down his face, and he could taste it all around his mouth. His hair clung to his forehead, his shirt stuck to his body, and his thighs screamed at the pressure he had to exert to keep himself in the chair.

He leaned back again, straining to pull the fish closer to the boat.

John watched the action at the end of the boat. "She's going to fly!"

Troy couldn't believe it. A huge fish, a monster, broke through the waves and flew sideways in the air, thrashing from side to side as it fought the hook in its mouth. Then as fast as it had come, it landed in the water and disappeared.

"*Yeehaw*!" Jason yelled. "It's a fucking monster!"

"Don't lose it, Troy!" John called out and came back to stand beside him. "This one's going to give you the fight of your life, son. You've got to listen to me and do exactly as I say if you want to land this bitch."

Troy nodded. His teeth were gritted so tight with effort, he couldn't speak.

"Don't forget to breathe. Sync your breaths to the fish. When you pull back, inhale deep. Exhale as you go forward, but slow."

Troy nodded again. Fuck. Now he had to concentrate on breathing too? It was hard enough pulling, cranking the reel, and feeling the fish through the pole.

But, man! What a rush! Jason was right. He'd never had an experience like this in his entire life. It was life-and-death. Man against fish. And there could only be one winner.

And by God, it was going to be Troy Hastings.

Troy set his teeth, wiped one hand on his shorts, grabbed the pole, wiped the other, grabbed the pole, and put his back into the next pull. Time slipped by as Troy fought the fish, lost in the intense concentration of the battle.

Minutes or hours later, he didn't know which, he heard John shout, "She's close! We've got her now!"

John moved out of Troy's line of sight, then returned with a long pole that had a wicked hook on the end. Must be the gaffing pole Jason had told him about, used to get the fish over the side of the boat and onto the deck.

"Come on, baby. You can land this bitch. You can do it." Jason stood by Troy's side, his eyes on the line as it zigzagged through the water. "I think she's coming up again."

She did. It was magnificent. As if in slow motion, the fish outlined against the blue sky, sunlight glinting off its shining scales, and the glitter of the millions of drops of water raining off the fish as it whipped its body back and forth, just about took Troy's breath away. Then she slammed back into the water and was gone.

He pulled back, then forward, cranking the reel, exhaling until the crank stopped and the sequence repeated. And repeated and repeated until Troy thought he didn't have any strength to give it.

The fish swam closer, and there seemed to be less fight in it. Less of those hard, deep pulls and more time where Troy just reeled it in, allowing him to get a second wind.

"She's broadside!" John leaned over the boat and grabbed the line with a gloved hand, his other hand holding the gaff. "Jason, get the second gaff. The short one. I'm gonna need help."

Jason left Troy's side, then reappeared next to John and leaned over the side, a shorter version of John's pole in his hand.

John said over his shoulder, "Now, Troy. Listen to me. I need you to lean forward just a bit and slowly crank the reel until I tell you to stop."

Troy unlocked his jaw. "Okay." He turned the reel slow, hearing the *click click click* of each crank. He couldn't see what was happening in the water on the other side of the boat, so he listened as the two men spoke.

"Jas, hook her just there. I'll get her in the gills."

"Here?"

"Right."

"Got her."

They leaned over, and Troy watched their asses as they worked as a team to get the big fish on board.

"Now?" Jason yelled.

John nodded. "Now!"

They heaved. Both men's backs strained, biceps bulged, thighs and calves tensing, they lifted the fish out of the water and, with a final yell, deposited it on the deck in front of Troy.

"Holy shit!" Troy gasped. The fish was nearly half the width of the boat. "How big is that thing?"

"Six feet, maybe. Two hundred pounds, give or take a few." John admired the fish as he squatted next to it and worked the hook out of its mouth.

"What is it?" Troy unbuckled himself from the chair and stepped down. His legs felt like rubber. He grabbed the chair to keep from falling over onto his catch.

"Tarpon. Great sport fish." John turned to him. "You did great, son. Just great. How'd it feel?"

"Fucking fantastic." Troy sighed and knelt down next to the fish. He ran his hand over its side, feeling the scales and taking in the beauty of the colors of its scales, bright and dark on top and then fading to white on the fish's belly.

"Damn, she's pretty." Jason placed his hand on Troy's shoulder.

"Yeah. She is." Troy stood and turned to Jason, then grabbed him in a huge bear hug. "Thanks, Jas. This is... It's..." he stuttered, unable to find the words. "Fuck. It's just great. Thanks."

"I know, dude. I almost cried when I caught my first big fish." Jason rubbed Troy's hair, sending sweat flying. "I'll get you a towel."

Troy nodded. "Thanks, John. I couldn't have done it without you."

"You did fine. You did it all. She's a keeper."

"A keeper?" What was he supposed to do with this fish? Weren't they going to eat it or something?

"She'll be beautiful mounted. Just think of her hanging on the wall over your fireplace." John grinned up at him.

Jason handed him the towel, and Troy ran it over his hair, neck, and chest.

"You know what this means, don't you?" Troy whispered.

Jason frowned. "No. What?"

"Tonight, your ass is mine."

Chapter Twenty-three

Troy sat back against the car seat and sighed. "I'm beat."

"Man, you should be. That fish was a beast! Two hundred and seven pounds." Jason whistled in appreciation.

"Sorry you didn't catch anything." They'd motored around the gulf for another two hours after Troy had caught his fish, but they'd had no luck hooking a second fish, so they called it a day and went back to Kemah.

"I can't believe you talked me into having that thing mounted." Troy groaned. "Where the hell am I going to hang it?"

"Over the bed?" Jason suggested.

"The bed?" Troy choked.

"Sure. Then you'd have to explain about how you met me and how I took you fishing and you caught it." Jason tapped Troy's thigh.

"Oh. So you want me to tell every man I take to my bed all about you?" Troy looked at Jason, hoping this was more of that possessiveness coming out.

Jason swallowed. Troy waited.

Jason shrugged. "Nah. I was just pulling your chain. Put it over the fireplace in your new place, dude."

Troy looked out the window. "That's what I was thinking. Over the fireplace."

They were so quiet all the way back to town that Troy fell asleep.

* * * * *

"I get the first shower." Troy closed the door behind him and started to strip off his clothes. They stank of sweat, fish, and seawater.

"Please!" Jason held his nose and waved his hand back and forth. "I thought I was going to choke in the car, dude. You've got a righteous stink working."

Troy rolled his eyes and headed to the bathroom. "You're not much better, Jas."

Jason grabbed a juice from the fridge, waited for Troy to disappear, then pulled out his cell phone. After scrolling through his numbers, he found the one he was looking for and hit Send.

With only one day left before Troy's friend Carlton returned, Jason didn't have much time left. This was his last idea, and it had better work.

He'd done all the adventure parts of his plan to give Troy the vacation of his life. Now it was time to pull out the heavy artillery.

The romance.

"Hey, it's Jason." He hopped off the couch and paced.

"Hey, dude! Long time no hear."

"Yeah, I know. Sorry I'm calling so late, but I've got a favor to ask. Do you have an opening for tomorrow morning?"

"Let me check the schedule."

Jason waited, his foot tapping on the floor, worried that Troy would come out before he finished making the arrangements.

"You're in luck. We had a cancellation. You want to book it?"

"Yes."

"How many?"

"Just me and my friend."

"Oh. Someone special? Should I make sure I pack the bubbly?"

"That'd be great, man." What could be more romantic? Maybe he should buy some roses too. Nah, that would just be overkill and look like he was trying too hard.

"The pickup point is at the big mall in Katy. Five thirty a.m. We'll be done by nine, okay?"

"Got it. See you then." Jason hung up, a huge smile on his face.

Troy came out of the bedroom, rubbing his hair with a towel, wearing only a pair of sweats. "Man, I'm starved."

"Look, it's Friday and I'm off tonight. How about a late dinner? Italian?"

"Pizza?" Troy frowned. "Or real Italian?"

"Real. Red tablecloths. Wine. Overpriced spaghetti."

"Sounds great. Shower's all yours." He waved at the bedroom.

"Thanks. Be out in a bit." Jason put his cell phone on the table and made a beeline for the bathroom.

If his plans to woo Troy worked, by this time tomorrow, Troy would want to stay longer.

Maybe forever.

* * * * *

"This place is really nice." Troy lowered his voice as he looked up from his menu and across the table for two at Jason.

Jason had been right. The restaurant was lovely. Gleaming silverware, candles on the tables, red cloth tablecloths, and a menu that didn't stop. Each item looked better than the next. "I'm having a hard time deciding."

"Well, I know what I'm having for dessert." Jason grinned.

"Did I tell you how good you look in candlelight?" Troy reached out and took Jason's hand.

"No. So tell me. How good do I look?"

"Good enough to eat." Troy licked his lips.

"Damn. Right here in the restaurant. Under the table?" Jason pretended to be shocked, but Troy saw the glint in his eyes. "Or do you want everyone to watch?"

"You'd like that, wouldn't you?"

"Yeah. It'd be hot, man." Jason took a sip of his wine. "But I'll behave tonight."

"Well, I hope you won't behave too much. Especially later."

"Later. About that." Jason cleared his throat. "I sort of planned something special for tomorrow morning."

"Breakfast?"

"Sort of. We need to wake up at four to get there at five thirty." Jason bit his lip and looked into Troy's eyes, searching for his reaction.

"No problem. After dinner, we can just skip the block and tackle I'd planned on setting up and go straight to the good stuff." Troy winked at him.

Jason laughed. "Sounds great. You don't mind that I made plans, do you?"

"No. Not at all." He touched Jason's hand again. "You've really spoiled me this week. You've been great, Jas. I've had the best time of my life."

"Really?"

"Really." Troy nodded.

For a moment, they gazed into each other's eyes. Troy wanted to say more, but he wasn't sure Jason wanted to hear it. No strings. Jason had set the rules, and until he said otherwise, those were the rules Troy would go by.

* * * * *

Jason took Troy's hand as they made their way from the car to the apartment. It was almost ten. Dinner had lasted longer than he'd planned, but they'd had so much fun talking about the fishing trip and learning more about each other, that they'd lingered until the waiters began giving them dirty looks and shutting down the restaurant.

Now Jason looked forward to having Troy all to himself in bed. He'd lost the bet and promised Troy his ass. It surprised him at how excited he was, how he couldn't wait to give in to his lover. He rushed to the door, put the key in the lock, and pulled Troy in after him.

"Hey!" Troy laughed as Jason pushed him toward the bedroom.

"Get in there. Strip. Now," Jason ordered. He might not be able to take the time to tie Troy up, but he wanted to enjoy as much time with his lover as he could. By now he knew they would both fall asleep after having sex, and with their early wake-up call, they wouldn't have time for anything in the morning. At least, not until they came back home.

"Yes, sir." Troy's eyes glittered, and he began undressing.

Jason stripped down, and together they climbed into bed. Jason pulled Troy to him, running his hands over Troy's firm body, cupping his plump ass.

"God, your ass drives me wild." Jason squeezed it.

"Hey, careful. You'll bruise the merchandise."

Jason rolled Troy over and licked a line down his spine. Troy shivered as Jason made his way lower, and that just turned Jason on even more. He loved that Troy was so responsive and that Troy quivered with desire for him.

Jason slapped Troy's ass, bringing a cry from his lover and a red palm print out on one cheek. "Fuck, that's beautiful," Jason whispered.

Troy looked back over his shoulder. "What, my ass?"

"Your ass. My handprint on your ass." Jason lowered his mouth to Troy's cheek and bit him, sucking up a love mark on it as Troy whimpered. "Damn. That's even more beautiful." He skimmed his hand over the mark.

"You like that, huh? Marking me?" Troy's eyes glittered with arousal.

"Marking my territory." Jason growled. "Let's other men know you're taken."

"Well, I haven't been taken yet. And besides, if anyone's ass gets taken tonight, it's yours, remember?"

"I remember." Jason sighed. "I've been thinking about it all day long. On the boat. In the car. At dinner." He took Troy's hand and pushed it into his erection. "See?"

Troy groaned and took Jason's dick in his hand and gave it a quick stroke, smearing precum over the fat head. "I see. Damn, Jas. You're so hard." The skin of Jason's shaft was soft as velvet covering a steel rod.

"For you, babe. Just thinking about you fucking me did it." Jason pumped into Troy's hand, his head back, and his eyes slitted like a cat enjoying a pet.

Troy let him go, reached for the condom and lube, and tossed them on the bed. Jason scooped up the tube of slick and squeezed some out on his fingers. Then, spreading his legs apart, knees in the air, he painted his hole with the lubricant as Troy watched.

"God, that's so hot." Troy gasped as he rolled on the condom. He was so hard, ached so badly, he thought he'd come right then. There was no need to prime the pump, he was ready to explode any minute.

"How do you want me?" Jason asked.

"On your hands and knees. I want to go deep." Troy edged back as Jason obeyed and rose up on all fours, presenting his ass to his lover.

"Damn, man. Your ass is prime." Troy leaned down and ran his finger through the cleft between Jason's firm globes, then lingered over his hole. He teased it, circling it, watching as it pulsed, as Jason clenched in anticipation of being penetrated.

Troy bit Jason on the cheek and left his own mark as Jason howled.

"Do it, man. Take me." Jason panted as he braced himself against the headboard. "Do it hard and rough."

"Sure?" Troy slipped his finger into Jason's tunnel. Jason grunted and pushed back onto Troy's finger.

"Yeah. Wanna feel it. Just do it."

Troy pulled out, placed the tip of his cock against Jason's entrance, and pushed all the way in. Both men grunted, panted, and shook as Troy held still, his cock buried balls deep in Jason's ass, then withdrew in a long, slow, slick slide.

"Oh goddamn. Fuck. Shit," Jason cried out as Troy's dick rammed back in. His body braced into the push of Troy's thrust, picked up the rhythm Troy set as he pumped in and out of his lover.

"Am I hurting you?" Troy ran his hand over Jason's back. Beads of sweat had gathered along his shoulders, and Troy wiped them away.

"No. It's so good. Fantastic." Jason shook his head and sighed, all the time pushing back into each of Troy's thrusts.

"Is this better?" Troy changed his angle and stroked over Jason's gland.

Jason cried out and slammed his fist into the headboard. "Fuck! Again!"

Troy nailed it again, and Jason shuddered. "Gonna come. I need more. Harder."

Troy had been holding back, trying to take it easy, but at Jason's insistence, he let go. As if the bindings had been cut, he felt a freedom unlike anything before, and he gave in to it. Hammering hard into Jason's ass, Troy's rapid strokes had him moments from losing his own load in the grip of Jason's tight tunnel.

The only sounds were their soft grunts, the slap of Troy's balls against the backs of Jason's thighs, and the soft, wet sound of his cock gliding in and out of Jason's hole.

Jason clamped down on him, and the incredible constriction around Troy's dick nearly locked him inside his lover. "Jerk off, Jas. Let me feel you come on me."

Jason reached up, and Troy watched Jason's arm moving, felt Jason's body tighten. Then, with a hoarse shout, Jason shuddered as he came.

Troy gritted his teeth as he rode the pulsing of Jason's muscles. It was so good, sending him straight to the wall, where he hung for what seemed like an eternity, then lost it and emptied into the condom. "Jas!"

The two lovers panted as they caught their breaths, then slumped to the bed, Troy on top of Jason.

"Sorry," Troy whispered. He'd move, but he couldn't seem to get his body to listen to his brain.

"About what? That was fucking fantastic, dude." Jason chuckled.

"You're in the wet spot." Troy rolled to the side with a groan.

Jason rolled over and ran his fingers through the drying cum on his belly. "It dries soon enough."

Troy caught Jason's hand and brought it to his lips. "Let me taste." He sucked two of Jason's cum-covered fingers in and licked them clean. "Delicious."

"Glad you like it." Jason grinned. "Now, can we go to sleep? Four a.m. is going to come around real quick." He rolled on his back and pulled Troy to him.

"I can't wait. I love surprises." Troy laughed.

"You're going to really love this." Jason smirked.

"Pretty sure of yourself, aren't you?" Troy rolled his eyes.

Jason wrapped his finger around the leather thong and pulled Troy to him for a kiss. God, there was just something about the way Jason did that, exerted his dominance over Troy, that made Troy feel so wanted. Like he belonged to someone at last.

But it wasn't at last. It was only for one more day. Then Jason would cut the thin strap of leather cording that bound him to Jason, and he'd be free.

He didn't want to be free.

He wanted to belong to Jason.

Troy nestled his head in the crook of Jason's shoulder and tucked his shoulder under Jason's arm. Jason wrapped his arms around Troy.

Well, if it wasn't going to last, at least Troy would enjoy what time they had together.

Chapter Twenty-four

"**W**ake up, sleepyhead," Jason whispered.

Troy grunted, "Go away," and rolled over. Jason sat up and smacked him over the head with his pillow.

"Hey!" Troy turned and landed a clean shot of his pillow against Jason's face.

Jason tossed it to the side, then fell onto Troy, grabbing his arms, and pinned him to the bed. He looked down into his lover's eyes.

Excitement, lust, hunger.

Fuck, he wanted Troy.

"What?" Troy asked, licking his lips. Jason watched as Troy's tongue slid over his full lips, leaving a shining trail of moisture.

"You know what." Jason took Troy's mouth in a savage kiss, pushing back

Troy's lips, forcing his way into his mouth and then sucking his tongue hard.

Troy moaned and humped into Jason's body, pressing his erection into Jason's belly.

"God, you woke up with a boner?" Jason chuckled.

"No. Shit. You do it to me." Troy blushed.

He fucking blushed. God, Jason couldn't stand it. He'd make up the time somewhere. He'd drive fast. Take the toll road. Hell, he'd run red lights.

He shimmied down Troy's body, grabbed Troy's cock, and swallowed it down.

Troy arched up, his hands clawing at the sheets. "Oh God. Jas."

Jason sucked him hard, flicking his tongue along the underside of Troy's shaft, tickling the bundle of nerves below the fat, dripping head. He loved the way Troy made those little whimpers, and the way the man tasted? God, it was addictive.

He'd fallen hard for Troy Hastings. So damn hard it scared him. He couldn't seem to pull away, even knowing it was going to come to an end soon.

"Gonna come," Troy warned.

Jason's hard cock begged for some attention. He grabbed his dick and jerked himself off as he gave Troy head.

Jason pumped up and down, applying suction as he pulled off Troy, then loose and wet going down on him. He worked his hand around and clutched Troy's balls. The sac crinkled at his touch; then the two choice nuts rose, and next thing he knew, Troy called out his name as he spilled a hot load down Jason's throat. Jason drank him down, savoring the bitter taste of his lover.

Unable to hold back, Jason came all over his own hand as ropy strings painted the sheets. He shuddered with the last hard shot, slowly pumping, bringing his tingling dick down.

"Fuck. Damn. Shit." Jason shook his head to clear it.

Troy laughed and threw his arm over his face. "Good morning."

"Yeah." Jason sighed. Then he sat up and slapped Troy on the shoulder. "I get first shower." He waved his sticky hand at Troy, jumped off the bed, and trotted to the bathroom.

"Jerk!" Troy tossed a pillow after him, but it hit the door as it closed.

* * * * *

"So where are we going?" Troy asked as he looked around at the businesses that lined the interstate heading west out of Houston.

"The mall."

"The mall. At five in the morning?" Troy stared at Jason like he'd gone nuts.

"You'll see." Jason grinned.

"This better be good." Troy crossed his arms over his chest.

Jason didn't reply. He'd let the surprise speak for itself.

They turned the corner of the big mall. A large shape loomed in the dimly lit parking lot.

"What is that?" Troy sat up and squinted through the windshield.

A flash from the gas flame, and its roar, gave away the secret.

"Oh my God! Is that what I think it is?" Troy bounced up and down in his seat.

"Well, if you're thinking it's a hot air balloon, you'd be right." Jason parked in a spot and had barely turned off the car before Troy had opened the door and leaped out.

"Oh my God." Troy stared at the balloon as it filled, rising off the ground. "Are we going up in that?" He turned to Jason, a look of pure excitement and joy in his eyes.

Thank God. He'd done the right thing. Jason said a quick thank-you to the gay gods.

"Come on. Let me introduce you to the owners of Up Up and Away hot air balloon rides." He led the way over to where two men and a woman stood next to the large basket.

"Jason!" The older of the men came forward, hand extended. Jason took it, and they shook. A beautiful young woman followed him, but the younger man hung back, tinkering with the balloon.

"Rob, this is my good friend Troy. Troy, this is Rob and his wife, Marla. They're the owners."

Troy shook hands and greeted them. "This is awesome. I've always wanted to do this."

"Jason said you're on vacation. And he said he wanted this to be special," Marla said. "So I'm going to ride with you, and Rob will drive the chase car with Simon driving the truck." She pointed to the younger man. He waved at them.

Troy and Jason waved back.

"The balloon will be ready in just a few minutes. In the meantime, let's get you guys on board." Rob slapped Jason on the shoulder and led them to the basket.

There was a small stepladder, and they climbed up it, swung their legs over, and settled in the basket. It was large enough to hold four or five people. In the center above them, the gas flame burned, sending hot air upward, keeping the balloon inflated.

After making a few equipment checks, Rob stepped back, released some lines, and the balloon lifted off from the parking lot.

"*Yeehaw*!" Jason called out, throwing his arm around Troy in a bear hug.

"Have you ever done this?" Troy asked. He stared down at the ground as it receded. The only sound was the burst of flame from the heater, but then silence. It was magical.

"Just once. It's incredible, man." Jason grinned at Troy.

"Where are we going?" Troy asked Marla as the balloon rose above the nearby buildings. "And how high will we be?"

She pointed west. "Two to five hundred feet most of the time, and we're headed out over the Katy prairie. We'll pass over subdivisions, but then there are some nice rice paddies and woods too." Then she ducked down and came back up with a bottle and two fluted glasses. "I understand this is a special occasion. We can't serve alcohol, but this has just as many bubbles."

She popped the cork and poured out sparkling grape cider, then handed them each a glass. "Now, turn around."

They did, and Troy gasped. The sun, a red-orange fireball, rose over the top of the city, sending streaks across the sky, painting it with bright, warm color.

Troy looked across his glass at Jason, then raised it in a toast. "To Jason. My hero. You helped me so much this week. Gave me back my life, really." Troy's voice wavered.

"Shit, dude." Jason shrugged, then raised his glass. "To Troy. I'm so fucking glad you didn't jump."

They stared into each other's eyes. Troy clinked his glass against Jason's, and they drank it down. The bubbles tickled as Jason swallowed, but he barely registered it. All he could feel was Troy's gaze, heating him up inside, warming him in a way no one had ever done.

Troy glanced at Marla as he hesitated.

"She's cool. She knows we're gay."

Troy exhaled. "Good. Will she mind if I kiss you?"

"Go ahead, guys. Just nothing that requires unzipping." Marla laughed and went back to steering the balloon.

Troy grabbed Jason by the front of his shirt and hauled him up against his chest.

"This is wonderful. I don't know how to thank you. The entire week has been fantastic, man." Then he plastered a kiss on Jason, fusing their mouths together.

Jason kissed him back, his hands cupping Troy's ass and pulling him tighter.

They broke apart when the need to breathe overcame them.

"I told you before, Troy. You don't owe me anything." Damn. Troy still felt obligated to Jason, and that's not what he'd wanted to inspire with this romantic ride.

Of course, it was foolish and stupid to think Troy would be so moved, so head over heels in love, that he'd lose it and shout out those three little words.

"I know." Troy looked down at his feet, then up out into the distance. "It's just beautiful up here." He leaned against the basket.

Jason stepped up next to him and leaned against his lover. "Yeah. Beautiful."

"Thanks for the best vacation ever, dude." Troy bumped his hip against Jason's hip.

Jason bumped him back. "Thank you. I had a great time too."

Troy rested his head on Jason's shoulder.

Marla sighed. "That's so sweet."

They turned to her. Jason raised an eyebrow. "What?"

"You guys. You're so great together." She smiled at them.

Troy looked at Jason. Jason bit his lip. "I uh, well, we aren't..." he stuttered. Man, he didn't want to explain their "no strings attached" agreement.

"There's nothing between us," Troy blurted out.

Marla looked at Troy, then at Jason, and shook her head. "Right. My mistake."

Jason picked up the bottle and filled their glasses again. "To Up Up and Away!"

"Hear! Hear!" Troy agreed, and they clinked glasses again, then downed the cider.

The ground silently slipped beneath them as the multitude of gray rooftops gave way to fields and woods.

Floating over the flat rice paddies, Marla pointed out a pair of eagles, several coyotes, and one or two herds of cattle. The only sounds were the occasional roar of the flame, the morning song of birds, and the whine of the interstate in the far distance.

As Troy relaxed against Jason, Jason wrapped his arm around his lover and held him close. He'd remember this week and this day in particular for the rest of his life.

He knew in his heart he did the right thing. It was true. He had to take a chance that in letting Troy go, Troy would embrace his new life and freedom and willingly return to Jason.

Chapter Twenty-five

The balloon landed in a field next to a two-lane blacktop highway just south of the interstate. The chase cars had parked there, waiting for them to arrive.

After the men on the ground wrangled the ropes and basket, securing it to the ground, Marla began the deflation process. Troy and Jason climbed out and stood back, watching the fully inflated, brightly colored balloon shrink down to flaccid silk covering the grass.

"Wow! Thanks, guys! I'll never forget this." Troy shook everyone's hand in his excitement. Then, for good measure, he hugged Jason again. It seemed he just couldn't keep his hands off the man.

While Marla opened a picnic basket filled with pastries and a thermos of hot coffee, the men quickly wrapped up the balloon and loaded the basket onto the back of the truck.

Once they'd eaten and each had a cup of coffee in hand, they climbed into the other SUV and headed back to the mall where they'd left Jason's car.

* * * * *

"I really need to find an apartment, Jason." Troy scrubbed his hand over his face. "Carlton will be back tomorrow, and I can get out of your hair then. But I'd like to at least be able to tell him I've found a place to stay." The pressure to have something settled had come out of nowhere, and it hit him like a full-on body slam.

Jason glanced over at Troy in the passenger seat. "You're not in my hair, dude. But I understand." He shrugged. "We can go home, grab your notes, and check them out. Unless you want to go alone?"

"Alone? Oh. Well, if you're tired, sure, I can go alone." Troy crossed his arms over his chest. Man, Jason really wanted him gone. That sucked.

"I'm not tired. I didn't say that, Troy." Jason exhaled. "I just wanted to give you some space."

"I don't need space," Troy barked. He knew what he needed. He needed for Jason to need him.

"Hey, man. It's okay. Relax."

Sure, Jason could be calm about this; it wasn't his house that had burned, not his life that was a smoking heap of shit.

"Don't tell me to relax," Troy snapped. "I've got to get out of here tomorrow, and I need a place to stay. I don't have any furniture or dishes, a bed, sheets, towels, mirrors, place mats, curtains, silverware, pots, pans—" Troy ranted, teetering on the verge of tears.

"Whoa! Dude, chill." Jason put his hand on Troy's thigh. "In time. It'll all be there in time. No one says you have to get all that stuff right away. Let's concentrate on the big shit first." He gave Troy a warm smile and a saucy wink.

Troy exhaled. "You're right. It's just that the time's almost up and I've got so much ahead of me. Finding a place is the easy part."

They pulled up to the apartment and got out. "Look. All your friends are going to be back tomorrow. Maybe they can help. Throw you a housewarming party or something."

Troy laughed. "Sure. I can register at Macy's, pick out really expensive crap everyone will trash me for picking, and then return what they give me for cash."

"Seriously. Do people do that?" Jason looked back over his shoulder as he unlocked the door.

"Brides do it all the time."

"What about gay guys who've been burned out of their apartments?"

"Not so much." Troy walked over to the table and picked up his list of possible apartments. "Got it. Let's go."

They left and drove to the first place. It was a large complex, but older and the rent was very reasonable.

"Looks nice," Jason said as they strolled to the rental office down a landscaped path off the parking lot.

Once inside, Troy introduced himself and asked to see the one-bedroom listed in the book. The manager was an older woman who gave them a hard stare, then took them to one of the buildings and up the stairs to the second floor.

"It's just been recarpeted." She unlocked the door and let them in. "I need first and last month's rent. Will that be a problem?"

Jason and Troy stood in the middle of the living room. The place was smaller than Jason's apartment and not nearly as nice. But it was closer to Troy's work.

"What's that smell?" Jason whispered.

"Cat piss," Troy whispered back. Aloud, he said to the manager, "I don't think this is big enough. Thank you for your time."

They left the apartment, jogged down the stairs and back to the car.

"Okay. One down. Three to go," Troy said as he got in the car.

"Dude. Please don't tell me you're saving the best for last." Jason shook his head. "Can't we just skip to it?"

Troy studied his notes. "Actually, there's one that just looks great, but it's a little more money than I used to pay. But it's bigger."

"Well, let's give it a try. If it's the one, it'll save a lot of time." Jason started the car and checked the address. "Hey, that's near my place." He glanced at Troy.

"Is it? I didn't notice that." Troy glanced up from the paper. "Is that a problem?"

"No, dude. It's cool." Jason shrugged.

* * * * *

They arrived at the complex and parked.

"This place is brand-new. I watched them build it. I thought the price would be sky-high, man." Jason looked up at the three-story old-world-styled brick building.

"It's a hundred and fifty more than my old place, but it's got more square footage." Troy read from his notes.

"You know, this place is about half a mile from mine."

"Huh." Troy grinned. "We're practically neighbors," Troy tossed out to see what Jason would say.

Jason didn't respond.

Shit.

They walked through a portico, across a cobblestone-paved courtyard with a huge but tasteful fountain in the center, and to the manager's office on the ground floor.

"Nice." Jason nodded his head. They stopped and checked out the Olympic-sized pool. "Hey, man, it has a hot tub."

"Nothing but the best for me." Troy laughed. "For the money they're asking, it better come with cabana boys."

"If it does, I'm hanging out here." Jason wiggled his eyebrows at Troy.

At the office, they went inside. The place had been designer decorated, and the manager greeted them and asked them to sit in two matching leather wingback chairs in front of her desk.

"Now. Are you looking for a place for the two of you? One or two bedrooms?" She smiled up at them as she placed a full-color brochure on the table.

They leaned forward as they read it. "No, just me," Troy answered.

"Okay." She tapped the brochure. "This is a popular floor plan. One bedroom with a study. One thousand square feet, master bath, Jacuzzi tub, walk in double shower, fireplace, built-in shelves, and space for a full-size washer and dryer."

"What fire prevention does it have?" Jason asked, going all firefighter and serious. God, it was so cute when he acted all protective. And damn sexy.

"All the apartments have smoke and carbon monoxide detectors, heat-sensitive sprinkler systems, and fire walls between apartments."

"Sweet." Jason nodded at Troy.

"I guess we should take a look." Troy stood, and Jason sprang to his feet also.

"I'll show you the model; then we can talk about where you'd like to be. Since we're so new, we're not fully rented and there's lots of choices. In fact, this month we're offering a special incentive—half off the first month's rent with first and last deposit."

"That sounds good." Troy glanced at Jason, who stuck up his thumb.

They followed her to the first floor of one of the buildings, and she unlocked the door. They stepped in and sank into plush carpet.

"Wow. Dude. This place is cracking." Jason whistled.

"It has wood floors in the kitchen and dining areas, carpet in the living room, bedroom, and study, and ceramic tile in the bath." She moved over to the fireplace and pointed to the built-in bookcases on either side.

"Look. There's room for the fish over the fireplace," Jason exclaimed.

"I see that." Troy nodded. Jason's face glowed as he walked around the large room.

"Let's check out the bedroom." Jason sprang to the door and threw it open. "Man, you gotta see this." Then he disappeared into the master bath. "Whoa! Troy! Take a look at this bathroom."

Troy laughed, shrugged at the grinning manager, and followed his lover through a spacious bedroom to the bath.

"Oh yeah, this is sweet!" Troy hadn't seen anything this plush except in a hotel. The tub and shower were to die for and most definitely big enough for the both of them. And it had a double sink. He ran his hand over the marble countertops.

"Man, you gotta take this place." Jason slapped him on the back.

Troy sighed. This was it. It had all the things he'd listed as must-haves. All it was missing would be Jason. "I'll take it."

"Great! Let's go back to the office, and you can pick out your building and floor."

* * * * *

Back at the office, they studied the buildings. Troy picked one close to the pool and on the second floor. "I can at least jump from there without killing myself."

Jason laughed. "This is true."

The manager produced a rental agreement and explained it, including the special price for the first month. This was it. Everything was perfect.

Almost.

She pushed the papers toward Troy to fill out and handed him the pen. "I need you to sign here, here, and here. Then initial here. Also, I'll need to make a photocopy of your driver's license."

Troy started writing. Previous addresses for the last five years. Next of kin. Work history. Five references. "Can I get back to you on these phone numbers? I lost my old cell phone, and I haven't programmed them in to my new one yet."

"Sure. I just have to have them before you move in."

"That won't be a problem," Troy assured her. Everyone would be back tomorrow, and he could get all the info then.

Finally, he'd filled everything out. All that was left was to sign it.

If he signed it, that was it. He'd be out of Jason's apartment, and to him that meant out of Jason's life. That was a good thing, right?

No. It still sucked.

Jason bit his bottom lip, his fingers tapping on the desk, and stared at Troy.

The print on the contract swam, the letters blurred.

"I don't want to do this," Troy croaked and pushed the papers away.

"What?" Jason whispered.

"I don't want to move out." Troy looked up into Jason's eyes.

Jason exhaled, fell back into the chair, and closed his eyes. "I can't believe it."

Shit. That's not what Troy wanted to hear. He wanted Jason to jump up, be excited, grab him, and hug him. He'd even settle for a sock in the arm.

"Maybe I should step out and let you two discuss this." The manager stood and left the office.

Troy stared at the man who'd been his lover for the last seven days. He opened his mouth to speak, then closed it. Jason had said enough for the both of them.

Jason opened his eyes. "Did you just say you don't want to move out of my place?"

"Yeah." Troy nodded.

"Oh fuck, man." Jason lunged across the gap between them and slammed into Troy, knocking him out of the chair and to the floor.

Jason pinned Troy down, their fingers interlocked, and stared into his eyes.

"You don't know how long I've been waiting to hear that."

Troy gasped, and Jason filled Troy's open mouth with his tongue, fusing their lips together. Oh God, could this actually be happening? Jason had *wanted* him to stay?

The manager opened the door and stepped in. "Is everything—" She squeaked. "Excuse me." Then quickly left, pulling the door closed behind her.

Troy grasped Jason's ass and pulled him close. Jason nipped Troy's lips, licked a soothing tongue over them, then broke away.

"I don't want you to leave. But I understand if you need to have your own place. This apartment is awesome, dude."

"Just knowing you don't want me to go makes all the difference in the world." Troy smiled as Jason rubbed their foreheads together.

"Take the place, babe." He fingered the leather thong. "You can take this off too, if you want."

"No fucking way. It's staying on until you cut it off me." Troy stared up into Jason's grinning face.

"Well, in that case, you're going to be wearing it for a long time."

There was a soft knock on the door.

The men scrambled to their feet as the door opened.

"Well?" She stepped in, went to her desk, and picked up the contract. "It's not signed." She frowned, her lips twisted in thought. "You know, this place is big enough for two. I have several couples renting these."

Troy glanced at Jason and raised his eyebrow.

"My lease is up in four months." Jason sat back in his chair.

Troy sat also. "So, if I sign this lease, will you move in with me then? Four months is a long time. A lot could happen in four months."

"I'll do better than that. I'll sign it with you, man. As a good-faith gesture." Jason grinned at him. "Go ahead. Take the place, if you want. Or if you want to live with me at my place, I want you there. Whatever you want, man."

Chapter Twenty-six

Carlton carefully placed the box he'd carried inside on Troy's new dining-room table. "Troy! Where do you want the dishes?"

Troy came out of the bedroom. "In the pantry closet." He pointed to the door just off the end of the kitchen counter. The Breakfast Club had helped him move into his new apartment, and now, Carlton helped him finish up.

His best friend carried it over to the counter and began unpacking. "I really like this pattern." He held up the new dishes and inspected them. "Simple, classy, elegant."

"Jason picked them out." Troy smiled.

"Jason, huh? That boy's got more going for him than good looks, a killer body, and a wicked taste for rope."

Troy blushed. "Shit, Carlton." He rolled his eyes. "I told you that in confidence."

"Everyone's gone home." Carlton laughed. "And I haven't told anyone. Swear." He held up his hand as if he were taking an oath.

"Not even Douglas?" Troy asked.

"Douglas?" Carlton snorted. "From what Mel told me, Dougie's eating his alley cat heart out."

Troy grinned and shrugged. "Too bad. He had his chance."

The door flew open. "I've got the fish, babe!" Jason announced as he lugged in the six-foot mounted tarpon. "Give me a hand, dude."

"Hey, babe." Troy scrambled around the boxes strewn over the floor to get to his lover. Together, they carried it over to the fireplace and leaned it against the wall.

Carlton put his hands on his hips and shook his head. "I can't believe you're going to actually hang that thing up in here." He shuddered. "It's so *butch*."

"Hey, I busted my ass landing that monster," Troy replied.

Jason grabbed Troy in a hug and planted a smack on Troy's lips. "Mm. My favorite flavor. Troy." He slapped Troy on the ass. "Hey, Carl."

"It's Carl-*ton*." Carlton shook his head. "When are you going to get it right?"

"Just jerking your chain, dude." Jason threw himself on the new leather sofa and tossed one of the pillows at Troy.

Troy caught it and tossed it at Carlton, hitting him in the belly.

"Hey!" he sputtered, looking very put out.

The guys laughed. "If you're hanging with us, dude, you're going to have to move a little faster," Jason said.

"I'm built for comfort, not speed." Carlton sniffed and went back to stocking the pantry with dishes.

Troy fell into Jason's arms on the couch. "Do you have time for some dinner before your shift at the station?"

"No. I need to get back to my place and shower. All this moving's got me sweating like a horse." Jason raised his arm. "Take a sniff, babe. I know you want to."

"Oh God." Carlton groaned. "The man's an *animal*." He rolled his eyes but couldn't hide his grin.

"I know. It's so hot." Troy laughed and leaned in to inhale his lover's scent.

"I can't believe you just did that!" Carlton gagged and pretended to throw up.

"You two are sickeningly sweet. My teeth might actually rot and fall out of my head."

"Jealous?" Troy asked.

"Intensely. Utterly." Carlton closed the box and put it on the floor. "I'm done. I'll see you tomorrow." He opened the door and paused. "And Troy? You finally got the man you deserved." With that, he waved them good night and left.

Troy turned to Jason. "Thanks for helping me get the new furniture set up."

"I didn't do much, just directed the furniture delivery guys, put the bed together, got lunch for all your friends, and then drove to Kemah to pick up your fish." He shrugged.

Troy glanced at the clock on the microwave in the kitchen. "How long can you stay?"

Jason hooked his finger under Troy's collar and pulled him so close, their lips met. "Not enough time to practice that new Shibari binding I learned."

"The one where my arms are tied between my shoulder blades?" Troy narrowed his eyes at his lover. Just the thought of being bound by Jason filled his cock. "The one in the photograph you showed me?" It had been one of the most erotic pictures he'd ever seen. Black-and-white, grainy, the bound man's skin had looked sweaty, perhaps from struggling against the rope, and smudged with dirt.

"I want to tie you up like that. Maybe take some photos?" Jason leered at him.

"Not if you're going to post them on the Internet, no way." Troy shook his head. Having his naked body tied up, out on the Internet for everyone to see, was going too far.

"Come on, man. It'll be hot." Jason nibbled along Troy's neck, around the cord.

"It will be hot enough having you bind me."

Jason pouted. "Okay, no photos." He looked so disappointed, like a kid whose scoop of ice cream had fallen off his cone and melted on the ground.

Troy sighed. "Well. Maybe just one or two. But you have to promise me they stay between us. No one else sees them, agreed?" God, what couldn't the man talk him into?

"Agreed!" Jason crowed and rubbed his hands together.

Troy grabbed a pillow and smacked his lover in the face. "Jerk."

"Dude." Jason wrestled Troy to the floor and pinned him down, pressing his hardness against Troy's thigh. "I have to go soon."

Troy lowered his voice. "Then don't waste any more time."

Jason's eyes lit up, his mouth twisted in a sexy smirk, and he shimmied down Troy's body. Within seconds, Troy's jeans had been unbuttoned, unzipped, and his cock released.

Jason stared down at the black ring that circled the base of Troy's swelling cock.

"Oh fuck! Did you wear this just for me?" He looked up into his lover's eyes.

"Just for you, babe. Like it?" There was nothing Troy loved more than the desire in Jason's eyes whenever he looked at Troy's body. Naked or clothed.

Jason moaned, then lowered his mouth and took the head of Troy's dick between his lips. His tongue lapped at the drops of precum oozing from its slit, and Troy bucked against him. Jason sucked it, then let it go with a soft *pop.*

"Like it?" He crawled up Troy's body and rested his forehead against Troy's. "Love it." He paused for a heartbeat. "Love you." Jason's uncertain gaze caught Troy's.

"Love you," Troy whispered.

"Dude." Jason sighed as he ran his fingertip over the leather collar.

"Jerk." Troy pulled Jason down into a hard, claiming kiss.

The End

Lynn Lorenz

Lynn Lorenz lives in Texas, where she's a fan of all things Texan, like Longhorns, big hair, and cowboys in tight jeans. She's never met a comma she didn't like, and enjoys editing and brainstorming with other writers. Lynn spends most of her time writing about hot sex with even hotter heroes, plot twists, werewolves, and medieval swashbucklers. She's currently at work on her latest book, making herself giggle and blush, and avoiding all the housework.

Find out more about Lynn by visiting her website:

http://www.lynnlorenz.com.

Made in the USA
Columbia, SC
01 July 2022

62582753R00161